Hj

THE
MAPMAKERS'
RACE

THE MAPMAKERS' RACE

EIRLYS HUNTER

ILLUSTRATIONS BY KIRSTEN SLADE

GECKO PRESS

For Madoc and Etta, with love

This edition first published in 2018 by Gecko Press
PO Box 9335, Marion Square, Wellington 6141, New Zealand
info@geckopress.com

Text © Eirlys Hunter 2018
Illustrations © Kirsten Slade 2018
© Gecko Press Ltd 2018

Distributed in New Zealand by Upstart Distribution upstartpress.co.nz
Distributed in Australia by Scholastic Australia scholastic.com.au
Distributed in the UK by Bounce Sales & Marketing bouncemarketing.co.uk

Gecko Press acknowledges the generous support of Creative New Zealand

Edited by Jude Watson
Design and typesetting by Katrina Duncan
Printed in China by Everbest Printing Co. Ltd,
an accredited ISO 14001 & FSC certified printer

ISBN: 978-1-776572-03-8
Ebook available

For more curiously good books, visit geckopress.com

CONTENTS

CHAPTER ONE

THE TRAIN

It really wasn't Joe's fault.

Ma had told him to be helpful, so when the train pulled into a station, he grabbed the empty flask and asked a man in railway uniform how long the train would stop for, and was there a tap? And the railway man looked at the clock and said eleven minutes, and outside the ticket office. Joe couldn't see a tap where the man said, but he found a pump at the horse trough out the front. He filled the flask, had a quick drink, then he pumped some water for a poor spaniel panting with the heat and was back at the train with two whole minutes to spare.

Sal was hanging out the carriage door. "Hurry, Joe. Run!"

He waved to Francie, whose anxious face was pressed to the window.

Then Sal said, "Where's Ma?"

Joe looked around. "What do you mean?"

"You were taking so long," Sal said, "she went to look for you."

"But I never get lost."

"She thought you must have gone exploring." Sal hovered with one foot on the step and one foot on the platform. "Where is she? Come on, Ma, it's about to go."

The train did a sudden jerk and steam swished up from around the wheels.

"It's going to leave!" She jumped back in.

Joe scrambled in after her and dropped the flask into the picnic basket. In the distance, doors slammed. Still no Ma. "Maybe we should get off?"

"Yes!" Sal's voice was panicky. "Let's get off—quick."

They'd been on the train since yesterday afternoon, and jackets, boots and socks, and bits of breakfast were strewn everywhere. Not to mention Humphrey, who was still fast asleep with his thumb in his mouth, and Carrot the parrot, perched on the luggage rack.

"Hurry, hurry, hurry!" Sal and Francie began to shove things into bags.

"Hurry, hurry," said Carrot.

Then Joe remembered. "But what about all our stuff in the guard's van?"

Too late. A whistle blew, someone slammed the door of their compartment, and the station started to move sedately past the window. Joe stuck his head out in case Ma was making a heroic leap for the last carriage, but she wasn't.

Their mother was left behind.

"No!" Sal flapped her hands. "Do something. Stop the train!"

Joe jumped onto the seat. He could just reach the red emergency handle above the door.

"Stop, wait!" Sal pointed to the words WARNING and PENALTY next to the lever. "What if they say it's *improper use*? *Fine: 20 sovereigns*. We haven't got any money. We might end up in prison."

She was right.

"What're we going to do?" She slumped down in a crumpled heap in the corner. "I told her not to go."

The train picked up speed, rushing them further and further from their mother.

Joe dropped into his seat next to Francie. "She'll catch us up. She'll get on the next train."

"But that could be ages," Sal wailed.

"Well, maybe she'll borrow a bicycle or a horse or something. I don't know. It'll be fine."

Francie was clutching her sketchbook to her chest. Joe always knew what his silent twin was feeling, and right now she was sending out waves of worry. He gave her a gentle shove.

"Really, Francie, she'll get on the next train. We'll be fine." Francie shook her head and opened her sketchbook.

Even though they had tried to be quiet, Humphrey woke up, scarlet-cheeked and rumpled. "The climbing train! Has it started?"

They had to tell him about Ma and he burst into a flood of snot and tears. Carrot flew down from the luggage rack and perched on his knee and pecked affectionately at his shirt buttons. Humph stroked Carrot's soft orange wing feathers and gradually calmed down. Sal dug about in Ma's holdall and found him a handkerchief.

"We're having an adventure, Humph," said Joe. "It'll be exciting."

"'Citing?" Humphrey narrowed his eyes. "'Citing? We'll see about that." Sometimes Humph seemed to go from being four to sixty-four at the speed of a shooting star.

When the guard came along the corridor Sal slid the door of their compartment open and asked him when the next train went to Grand Prospect.

He leaned in the doorway. "This is just a once-a-week service at the moment, miss. Should be going daily before winter, though."

They sat like statues until the man had moved away, then they exploded together, *"A week!"*

Humphrey threw himself at Sal and wound his arms around her neck. "I want Maaàaaaa!"

Francie clutched her stomach. "Francie feels a bit sick," said Joe.

"Me too," said Sal. "I feel as if I've swallowed a mouse and it's trying to scratch its way out of my tummy."

"T-r-u-b-l," said Carrot.

"But Ma probably won't wait for another train. She'll get a ride on a cart, or perhaps there's a stage-coach." Joe tried to sound as if he believed himself. "It can't be much further to Grand Prospect."

The train sped on and on. Francie hunched over her sketchbook and drew pictures of their old home. Humph sucked his thumb and sniffed sadly as tunnels and bridges, fields, farms and forests flashed past the window.

Joe tried to swallow the lump in his throat. "It's too far, isn't it?"

He couldn't imagine what might happen next. None of them had ever spent so much as a night without their mother.

"What about the race?" said Sal quietly. "It's our last chance."

They were going to Grand Prospect for the Great Mapmakers' Race, and their whole future depended on winning. Their mother was a brilliant mapmaker, but no one wanted to employ her without their father, who was an explorer and route-finder. When Pa hadn't come back from his last expedition, Ma had taken a job cleaning a beer house, but the landlord said her scrubbing wasn't up to scratch and sacked her. No job meant no money for rent, so at the beginning of summer the Santanders left their house and moved into their tent, which they all preferred anyway, but Ma said winter would be another story.

Joe earned a few coins helping the bee woman move her hives from the orchard to the water meadows, and they all worked for a few days thinning apples, but the money had soon run out. In desperation, Ma spent the last of their savings on the entry fee and supplies for the Great Race to find and map a route over the mountains from Grand Prospect to New Coalhaven. They wouldn't be a family any more unless they could win a share of the prize money.

The guard walked along the corridor ringing a bell and shouting, "Secure your belongings, sit back in your seats. Ascending the Vertical in five minutes. Five minutes to the Vertical."

Sal looked stricken. "I'd forgotten about the Vertical."

They'd all been so excited about going on a climbing train, but now the only feeling they had room for was worry. Sal stood on the seat and the others passed up their loose belongings to shove behind the net in the luggage rack, then the guard came through again and ordered them to sit tight. He released the latches that unlocked the rear-facing seats so Sal and Humph were tipped backwards and their legs shot up, like being in a dentist's chair. Humph waved his feet at Joe. The train shuddered and clanked. Humph looked worried.

"They'll be taking the engine off," said Sal.

"Where?" asked Humphrey. "Why?"

"They don't need it. The carriages caterpillar up while the engine turns around on the turntable. There'll be another engine waiting at the top. You'll see."

There was a tremendous jolt—and they were off.

Up and down the train people were yelling and screaming as the track got steeper. The Santander family were yelling, too, though they were more exhilarated than scared, and Carrot joined in for an excuse to screech. Francie and Joe, facing forward, could see how steeply the carriage was sloping up; Sal and Humph could mostly only see the ceiling and the sky.

"We're like a fly crawling up a wall," said Joe.

"The train only goes to sixty-seven degrees; walls are ninety." Sal was the sort of person who minded about the difference, but the others couldn't care less about the maths. They were in a climbing train, and for a few minutes the thrill of the Vertical blotted out everything else.

Looking down, Joe could see tiny roofs and treetops—and then suddenly the window was filled with another train, travelling in the opposite direction.

"Counter-balancing," said Sal, with satisfaction.

The people in the other train had their mouths open and looked petrified.

Then it was gone and there was just a glimpse of its guard's van vanishing into the distance far below. Too soon the track levelled out and the carriage went back to its regular angle and slowed to a stop.

"Again!" shouted Humph. "Let's go on it again."

"Poor Ma, she was so looking forward to the Vertical. It won't be nearly as much fun for her on her own," said Sal.

"And Pa," said Joe. "Pa would have loved it."

He tried not to think about Pa too much because he ended up with an ache in his middle, so he made himself think about something else.

"When does the race actually start?" he asked.

Sal unpinned the letter of confirmation from the lining of the picnic basket where Ma had put it for safekeeping. She read: "*All expeditions will depart at 10 am on Saturday the tenth ...* Blah blah *... and thereafter ... forfeit entry to the race if not departed by midday*. Saturday. Tomorrow. By midday. So that's it." She crossed her arms over her chest as if she were trying to hold herself together. "I'll have to be a housemaid. A life of servitude. I knew it."

That made Joe snort with laughter because Sal couldn't toast a piece of bread in front of the fire without burning it, and when she was doing the washing up she'd just let go of the plate she was drying if she had an interesting mathematical thought. Ma usually kept her away from the dishes.

"Well, I'm not going to be a servant," said Joe. "I'll be a nomad if I can't be an explorer. And Francie will be an artist."

Francie nodded. She never spoke, but Joe and Francie's thoughts often got mixed together and Joe had spoken for both of them since they were very small. She drew instead of speaking, and she needed a pen or pencil in her hand like other people needed air in their lungs.

Sal bit her lip and stared at the telegraph wires swooping past, with a counting look on her face. Joe nudged her leg with his foot.

"You know what? We can still enter the race. If we set off with the other teams tomorrow, we can stop as soon as we're outside Grand Prospect and wait for Ma to catch up."

"What'll we eat?"

"We've got sacks full of food. And it doesn't all need cooking."

"Raisins don't," said Humph, in a small voice.

"True. Nor does salt." Sal's chin wobbled and she looked as though she were going to burst into tears, but she started to laugh instead, and her crazy whooping set Joe and Francie and Humphrey off, too. For a minute, it was just like the old days before Pa disappeared—falling about and laughing together until their sides ached.

No parents, no money, no home—what else could they do?

CHAPTER TWO

THE SANTANDER TEAM WILL START TOMORROW

Even though Grand Prospect was the end of the railway line, Sal wasn't taking any chances. She made them put on their socks and boots, and get everything packed up and ready by the door so they could jump out as soon as the train stopped.

Grand Prospect Station was just a raised wooden platform in a field of bare dirt. People poured off the train with baskets and boxes. A ramp was lowered from the stable carriage and a group of men filed out, each leading a horse, skittering and snorting, onto the platform. The men were wearing riding boots, big-brimmed Stetson hats, bandanas around their necks, and leather waistcoats with a symbol on the back showing a rifle and a telescope crossed over a map. Another team. Sal bit her lip. They looked so professional.

"I bet they're the ones Ma calls the Cowboys," she whispered to Joe.

The guard's van doors opened and the guard began dumping out bags and bundles. Immediately there was a bellow from the tallest Cowboy, a giant of a man.

"You break anything and I'll break your neck," he growled.

The guard backed out of the way, and the big man climbed into the luggage van and passed out saddles and saddle-bags to his companions, who buckled them onto their horses. Then he mounted his horse and wheeled it in a tight circle, almost trampling Humphrey.

"Hey! Watch out!" Sal yelled, snatching Humph away from the clattering hooves.

The man looked at her, eyes narrowed to a slit. Then he spat, and the wad of tobacco he'd been chewing landed at her feet. "You should take care now, girly." He kicked out and the heel of his boot grazed Sal's arm.

"Ouch! You, you—" Sal tried to think of a word that sounded angry enough.

"You, you!" Humphrey shouted after the men, who were cantering off in a cloud of dust.

Sal had to forget the Cowboy because everything from the guard's van was piling up on the platform. She and Joe dragged the bundle of tent canvas to one side and stacked the rest of the family's belongings next to it: rucksacks, tent poles, surveying equipment and sacks of food. The other passengers strode off, and porters trundled after them with trolleys loaded with crates and trunks; everyone else in the whole world seemed to know just where they had to be and what they had to do next. Sal perched on a kitbag.

"We can't possibly carry all this stuff. What are we supposed to do now?"

"I know," said Humphrey. "Let's have dinner."

"We haven't *got* any dinner," Sal said, more fiercely than she meant to.

"Hey. You kiddies." A man carrying a huge ledger book bustled across the empty platform towards them. He said he was the mayor's assistant and demanded to know who they were.

Sal stood up as straight as she could and smoothed her skirt. Her heart was thumping. "Good afternoon. We're the Santanders. I'm Sal, this is Humphrey, and Francie and Joe."

The assistant looked doubtful. He consulted his ledger. "Santander. That name is in my register, but I am looking for Angelica and Leopold. Their dray is waiting."

"Our mother and father have been, um, delayed a little. They'll be here very soon." Sal hated lying and didn't think she sounded convincing.

"No, they won't, cos they're—" Humph began, but Joe towed him away to look for the grappling hooks under the train.

The mayor's assistant looked at Sal and Francie as though they were something nasty-smelling on the sole of his boot. "Your parents may do as they please, of course, but the race begins tomorrow. The dray over there was ordered to convey the Santander expedition to the square. The feast begins at five sharp."

He stuck his nose in the air and hurried off.

"Feast! Joe, Francie, did you hear that? There's a feast!" Sal suddenly felt very hungry. They wouldn't starve to death tonight, at least. "And a dray, whatever that is."

The dray turned out to be a kind of cart, pulled by an enormous carthorse, and driven by a beanpole of a red-headed boy called Beckett, who was wearing a shirt with sleeves that barely reached his elbows, flapping trousers held up by a string belt, and a fraying straw hat. He helped them heave the heavy tent on board.

He held out a finger to Carrot and didn't wince when she pecked at it.

"Beautiful bird."

Carrot put her head down and tickled his hand with her green crest.

"She likes you," said Joe.

"Smart as well as beautiful, then."

"S-m-r-t," Carrot spelled.

Beckett laughed. "Nearly!"

When everything was loaded, he said they could all sit on the driver's bench with him if they didn't mind squashing. Sal hung on to Humphrey, who was very interested in the horse.

"He's so big. What's he called?"

"Well, I call him Plodder." Beckett had a slow way of speaking.

"Why?" asked Humph.

"To encourage him, poor beast," said Beckett.

The cart rattled out onto a wide dirt road and they headed into town. Sal hadn't realised how big and grand a town could be. Six, seven, eight blocks already. And the buildings looked so important, with their shiny signs saying *The Daily Bugle* and *Mechanical Mining Machinery Co. Ltd* and *New Territories Savings Bank* in fresh bright paint.

Humphrey kept squealing and demanding, "What's that?"

"He hasn't been anywhere like this before," Sal explained. "None of us has."

"Grand Prospect's growing fast," said Beckett. "See the clock tower? It's brand new. The green roof behind is the technical school. And see the yellow smoke? That comes from the vulcanizing factory, and the black smoke comes from the Progressive Metal Foundry."

Sal exchanged looks with Francie. Francie obviously hated the sulphurous smell and the gritty dust as much as she did.

"Are you folk actual explorers?" asked Beckett.

Joe explained. "Ma and Pa are, but they stopped racing when we were born so this is our first real race. But we've done loads of mapping—we mapped the Nerys Islands with them, and the Dorland Alps. And we did the Talbert Traverse when Humphrey was a baby."

"Heck!" Beckett sounded properly impressed.

"I was only little," said Humphrey.

"So where are your parents now?" Beckett asked.

"They—" Humphrey began, but before he could explain, Sal gripped his arm.

"Shh! You mustn't tell people. Else we might not get dinner."

"We'll all get dinner, I'll make sure of it," said Beckett. "I've heard about this race. It's to find a route through to New Coalhaven, isn't it?"

Sal repeated what their mother had told them. "It's because of all the coal mines there. The only way to get the coal out and supplies in is by boat. But the port is too dangerous. There are rocks and sandbanks, and lots of ships get wrecked. The race is a competition to find an overland route, first for a horse track, but then for a railway."

"A railway?" Beckett pushed back his hat and narrowed his eyes. "This competition is to find a route for a railway from here through to New Coalhaven?"

"Yes," said Sal. "I just said."

"A railway! A railway through the mountains." Beckett grinned. "I think that might just change everything."

"Why does it?" asked Humph. "What does it change? Why?"

"I need to do some thinking—then I'll tell you." Beckett's voice was drowned out by the thunder of a load of logs being tipped off a cart.

Francie shuddered and put her fingers in her ears. Grand Prospect was too noisy. There were people everywhere, busy, busy, busy, and this part of the town still seemed to be under construction, with stacks of timber on every corner, and lots of shouting, sawing and banging.

Beckett beamed. "At this rate, Grand Prospect's going to be a city in a year or two. What a place!"

They all looked at him.

"You like this noise and all these people?" Sal was astonished. Beckett seemed a perfectly ordinary, nice person—how could he possibly like this town?

Beckett nodded. "Certainly do! It's progress. It's the future unrolling." And he turned Plodder into the town square.

*

The square was criss-crossed with strings of coloured bunting, and a stage had been built at one end. It looked very important. There were more people milling about than Sal had ever seen in one place.

Beckett stopped the dray next to a statue of a frowning man in a top hat who was pointing at the sky. Joe and Humph climbed down and went to investigate a long table covered with piles of food under white cloths, but a red-faced man bellowed at them, "Hey you! Speeches first."

They came slinking back.

From the top of the dray, Sal had a good view of the people sitting on the stage, the women in wide hats, and the men in tall hats and tail coats.

First the mayor and then the chairman of the Railway Company spoke about Heroic Endeavour, Glorious Railways, the Challenge of Gradients, and the Miracles of Modern Steam Power. He went on and on. Sal yawned. Joe and Humph were trying to balance on the top rail of the fence around the square, Beckett's eyes were closed, and Francie was drawing Carrot, who was dozing on Beckett's shoulder.

Finally, the chairman finished and the crowd applauded in relief, but the mayor stood up to speak again.

"Let me remind you of the extraordinary prizes being offered in this unique competition."

Sal called to Joe to come and listen.

"The first team to arrive in New Coalhaven will receive five hundred guineas." The crowd clapped and the mayor nodded graciously. "In addition, the team that produces the best route for a horse track, complete with maps, will receive one thousand guineas." The crowd cheered. "AND if their route proves suitable for a railway line, they will receive a further two thousand guineas, provided—" he held up his hand for silence, "they arrive at the finish line before sunset on St Solitude's Day, twenty-eight days from today."

Sal gasped. Twenty-eight days! Actually no, only twenty-seven from tomorrow. Just finding a route could take twice that long, let alone surveying it—no wonder they could offer such a huge prize. So little time. But so much money. If they won they'd easily have enough money to buy a boat and sail off and search for Pa.

If only Ma had trusted Joe and stayed on the train.

The mayor picked up a pile of envelopes. "And now, the team leaders will come up to receive their race instructions. First up, please welcome Roger Rumpledown, team leader of Roger's Ruffians."

Roger Rumpledown stumbled up the steps, smiling and waving at no one in particular. He took the large envelope the mayor gave him and ignored the hand being held out for him to shake.

Sal hadn't realised someone might have to go up onto the platform in front of everybody. Her knees suddenly felt too wobbly to take her anywhere.

"Next, it is my privilege to introduce you to the world-renowned explorer, Mr Cody S. Cole the Third, leading his team Cody's Cowboys."

There was a stir as the crowd parted for Cody S. Cole III. It was the tobacco-spitting giant from the train. He sauntered onto the platform, shook the mayor's hand and took his envelope.

"Cody Cole is serious competition," Sal said. "Do you remember Ma and Pa talking about him, Joe? They beat him by a whisker in that race to find a route through Lauratia."

"And next I'd like to introduce the Solemn Team, which stands for the Society of Logical Explorers, Mappers and Navigators, led by Mr Keith Skinner. These men are scientific!"

A thin young man who had been doing star jumps at the back of the crowd ran forward, took his envelope and nodded a tiny bow.

Carrot scratched her head with a long claw. "Hip, hip, hoo. Hip, hip, hoo."

"And now, it is my great honour to introduce to you Sir Montague Basingstoke-Black, leader of Monty's Mountaineers."

Sir Monty heaved himself out of a folding chair and climbed the steps to the platform in a cloud of pipe smoke. His team all had pipes clamped between their teeth. They called out "here here" and "jolly good show".

"Isn't he the one who crossed some desert and found that ruined city?" Beckett whistled. "He's famous."

Joe nodded. "The Desolo Desert. But our Ma says Sir Monty spends so much time being a World Famous Explorer nowadays that he's stopped doing actual exploring. With a bit of luck, he'll have forgotten how."

The mayor cleared his throat. "And next, in the spirit of a new age, we have the ladies from the Association of Women Explorers. Mind you're not AWE-struck, gentlemen!"

Some of the men in the crowd laughed, and a woman wearing a white dress and a sun hat as wide as a carriage wheel cleared a path for herself by waving a walking stick in front of her.

"The name is Agatha Amersham," her voice boomed out. "*When* we win this race, we will use the prize money to endow a college for young women to study surveying and engineering."

The crowd cheered and jeered in equal numbers.

Sal stared. "I didn't even know they were things you could study." She jabbed Joe. "Did you know that?"

"Shh—listen."

The mayor peered at his notes. "And finally, the Santander family."

People looked around.

"No show by the Santanders?" said the mayor. "In that case we move on to—"

Sal had to be brave. "Wait!" She took a deep breath, jumped off the dray and scuttled through the crowd to the platform. She wiped her hand on her skirt and stuck it out for the mayor to shake.

"MynameisSalvatoraClementinaElsieMaySantander."

"I beg your pardon?" He raised an eyebrow and looked down his nose at her.

The crowd laughed.

She tried again more slowly, though her mouth was dry and she felt hot and prickly under her skin. "My name is Salvatora Clementina Elsie-May Santander."

The mayor towered over her, even though Sal stood as tall as she could. "Is this a joke?" he boomed. "First, a team of women, and now a team of children. It's ridiculous. This is emphatically *not* a race for juveniles."

"The Santander family will be racing." Sal's voice wobbled but she spoke very loudly so everyone could hear. "Our parents are delayed right now, but you confirmed our entry. The Santander team will start tomorrow."

CHAPTER THREE

CREAM CAKE
AND
JELLIED EELS

"Brilliant! You did it!" Joe gave Sal a hand up onto the dray. He hugged her and Humph did too. "Santanders forever!"

Sal huffed out a big breath that set her fringe fluttering. "That was terrifying!"

"But you showed that horrible mayor." Joe laughed. "We're still in the race!"

Sal gave the envelope to Francie. "You never lose anything so you'd better look after it."

Francie nodded and slipped the envelope into her sketchbook.

"That was brave," said Beckett.

"Thanks!" Sal looked embarrassed but pleased.

"It must be food time, now. I could eat fifty feasts." Joe jumped off the dray but before he could get to the food table, a hand reached out of the crowd and clamped down on his shoulder. It squeezed too hard to be friendly.

"A junior Santander!" Cody Cole sneered at Joe. He was chewing slowly, and he wasn't smiling. "What d'ya think, boys? A bit scrawny, but I guess a hungry wolf ain't that fussy?"

The other Cowboys laughed, and one of them started to howl like a wolf.

"You'll meet wolves and worse out there," Cody Cole drawled. "Best trot home on your hobby horse, kiddo."

Joe found that he knew just what to say. "You must think we're serious competition, else why would you bother to try and frighten me?" He wriggled free and shouted, "Thanks for the compliment!" as he ran off.

Who cared about the stupid Cowboys? The covers were being lifted off the food at last. But immediately the table disappeared behind a wall of explorers and organisers, leaning and reaching and filling their plates. And there they stayed, talking and eating.

Sal joined Joe behind the row of backs. "Excuse me," she called. "Hey! Excuse me!" but everyone behaved as if they were invisible.

"My tummy can't wait another minute," said Joe. "Let's go caving."

He bent down and pushed between the black woollen trouser legs and rustling skirts until he was under the long table, which was made of planks resting on trestles. Sal squeaked "No!" but she followed. Joe pulled an empty flour sack out of his pocket and gave it to her to hold, then he reached up around the table-cloth and ran his fingers along the edge of the table until they felt something. He lifted it down carefully. A bowl of plums. He put one in his mouth and tipped the rest into the sack. Sal added a

plate of sandwiches. Fishpaste! They clambered over the trestles and crept under the length of the table, snaffling vegetable fritters, hard-boiled eggs, slices of beef, a plate of buttered bread and a tray of cheese tarts as they went. Then Sal lifted down an oozing cream sponge.

"I'll take it separately," she whispered.

They crawled out right near the Solemn men. "What have you heard about the Santanders?" Keith Skinner was saying, as he hacked at a ham.

"He died," said one.

"She walked out," said another.

"One of the girls is doolally. Completely dumb."

"No competition there, then!"

They snorted and sniggered—until Sal thrust the cream cake at Joe and seized a dish of jellied eels in both hands.

"Liars! That's not true at all," she gasped, and upended the eels over Mr Skinner's knickerbockers. Then she picked up the ham and shoved her way out through the crowd.

Joe followed, clutching the cake and the bulging sack and laughing so hard he nearly dropped everything.

He was laughing too much to explain, so Sal had to tell the others.

"That Mr Skinner will surely reek," said Beckett approvingly.

When he was absolutely full, Joe licked his fingers. He stretched and lay back on the dray next to Francie, who had a cream moustache. "Best picnic ever. And loads of leftovers."

"Which is just as well," said Sal. "Seeing as how Ma took her purse with her."

Joe was jumping up and down like one of the Solemns, trying to make room for a second slice of cake, when Roger Rumpledown wandered over, nodding like a buoy on a bumpy sea.

"If it isn't Santander's brood, by jove!" he shook his head. "Sad business. Sad, sad business." He smelled vinegary, like The Jolly Swagman before Ma had mopped the floors.

"I'm not sad!" Humphrey said. "I'm going 'sploring to New Coalhaven."

"Dear little fellow." Roger ruffled Humphrey's hair and shambled off again, mumbling, "What a waste. Short life."

Sal was furious. "They're all at it. I wanted to ask Agatha Amersham about her college but she just said, 'A mapping race is no place for children, my dear, go home.' And Sir Monty blew pipe smoke into my face and called me a brainless idiot. None of them think we can do it. We'll show them!"

She packed up the picnic with great ferocity, slamming down tin lids and slapping out cloths.

"Oy. You." A grumpy-looking middle-aged woman hailed

them from the road. She was leading two skinny horses. "You know Angelica Santander?"

"She's our mother." Joe climbed onto the railing to talk to her. "We're the Santander team."

"Well, where is she?"

Joe stroked the nose of one of the horses. Its eyes were yellowish and sticky. "She's held up. She'll be here in a day or two."

"She ordered two horses and three sovs' worth of dried food. Meat, fruit, vegies. You better give me my money."

This was awkward. And she hadn't finished.

"Plus, the hire of the horses and the deposit. Fifty-three all up."

Sal leaned on the fence, her mouth hanging open. "Fifty-three sovereigns? But we can't—"

"Sorry," said Joe, "we haven't got any money. Not so much as a penny."

The woman turned on Sal. She looked as if she were about to explode with rage, and gobs of spittle flew as she shrieked, "Cheats! Liars! Shouldn't be allowed. I'll get the organisers onto you."

Sal went rigid; people were staring. Luckily Beckett came back just then. He knew what to say about the horses and he said it in his slow, peaceable voice:

"Hello, you two. What sad old nags. Poor things, too weak to even flick away those flies."

The woman blustered some more, but a man who'd been watching called out that those horses would have a hard time getting back to their paddock, let alone over a mountain. And when Sal promised, cross her heart, that Ma was coming, and would pay for the food, the woman clomped away, dragging the reluctant horses after her.

Beckett saw Sal's face. "Don't worry, there's plenty of folk with money around here. They'll buy her food and she'll end up getting paid twice. But I've scrounged some for nothing."

He'd been helping to clear the tables and been rewarded with two loaves of bread, a wheel of cheese, two pork pies (hardly started), a currant pudding, most of a jar of pickled cucumbers and a small sack of apples to add to their supplies.

"Oh my goodness, thank you! This'll feed us for a week," said Sal.

He looked doubtful. "Three days, perhaps."

"But what exactly are we going to do now, with no pack-horses?" Joe considered their baggage from every angle. "Can we just carry what we need?"

Beckett laughed. "If you were the Hercules family, maybe."

Francie emerged from behind the tent canvas where she'd been hiding away from the shouting. She tried to lift the sack of tent poles. Heavy.

"How about donkeys?" said Beckett. "I know a man who has some donkeys."

"I like donkeys," said Humphrey, sharing an apple with Carrot.

Beckett had one condition. "I can borrow some donkeys for you, right enough, but I'll have to come with you to look after them."

Sal shook her head. "You can't. It's too dangerous."

"Dangerous?" Beckett hooted. "Do I look like a mollycoddled mumpkin?"

Sal's cheeks turned beetroot red. "It's just, I don't know—Ma, what she'll say—we need to ask—"

"Ma needs to make the important decisions, not us," Joe explained.

"But she isn't here, is she?" Beckett looked at the heap of baggage on the dray. "It's simple. We take the dray, go to my village, I borrow us some donkeys, then we'll be all ready to go over the mountains when your mother catches up."

"Mollycoggled mumkin!" Humph chuckled around his thumb.

"Why would you want to?" Sal demanded. She'd climbed onto the dray and was pulling the bags about as though she expected them to decide for themselves which could be left and which must be taken. "Most people seem to want to stay at home, not go exploring. And you said that you'd come to Grand Prospect to earn money for your family, which you won't be doing if you come over the mountains."

"Unless we win," said Joe.

"Unless we win."

Beckett stroked Plodder's neck. "Well, the first reason is, I've been having a closer look at those other teams and they're all pompous asses. It would be a right shame if one of them won all that money."

"Pompous asses!" Humph danced around the dray. "Pompy, pompy, pomp."

Sal rolled her eyes at Beckett. "And?"

"And I reckon it's past time I had an adventure."

"And?"

"I want a railway. I really, really want a railway."

CHAPTER FOUR

OVER THE BRIDGE

Joe was exhausted, but he couldn't sleep. The Milky Way was a bright brushstroke arcing high overhead. The longer he looked, the more stars he could see, glittering hard and icy. One day he'd have a telescope of his own, and he'd stay up all night and study the secret patterns of the stars. He'd learn to find his way by following the star roads.

He wondered how far it was over the mountains and how high they were. And about Ma and Pa. And then he had a genius thought.

He nudged Sal. "Sal? Do you think we can do it?"

Sal rolled over in her sleeping bag. "Ma thought we could."

"But without Ma, I mean," said Joe.

"On our own? That's the stupidest idea you've ever had."

"I can find the route, no problem."

"No. We can't."

"And Francie can draw the maps." Francie's fingers found Joe's hand in the dark and squeezed yes. "It makes sense," said Joe. "We've only got twenty-seven days from tomorrow, which is an impossibly short amount of time, and if we wait for Ma it might only be twenty."

"But … no adults?" Part of her wanted to try, he could tell.

"Beckett's nearly an adult. And you can do the calculations and manage the altimeter, can't you?"

"Yes, but—" She was wavering.

"I was going to find the route anyway. Francie was going to draw the maps anyway. What else is there?"

"But—"

"We know how," Joe insisted. "Instead of just getting the donkeys then waiting for Ma, we should get the donkeys and keep going. If that's all right with Beckett."

"He likes towns!" Sal hissed, as if he'd admitted to drinking blood.

"He's tall and strong. And he's nice."

"I suppose if we set off at least we'd have a chance." She began to sound a little bit excited. "And Ma could catch us up."

"When we win we can go and look for Pa," said Joe.

"What about the wolves?" Sal whispered.

"High mountains," Joe whispered back.

"Extreme weather conditions," said Sal.

"Nothing to worry about then," they said together, and they laughed—but quietly so as not to wake Humphrey.

"Twenty-seven days," said Joe, and he rolled over and went to sleep.

The new town clock chimed ten times then the mayor blew his whistle.

"I don't know about this," said Sal. The mouse in her stomach felt bigger this morning—more like a ferret or a weasel. "I really don't know about this."

It was time for the teams to leave. The mayor pulled their names from his hat, and first to trot over the bridge was Cody

Cole and his six Cowboys. All their faces were shadowed by their big Stetson hats; they held the reins of their horses in one hand and leaned back in their saddles as they rode, their other hands resting near the shiny revolvers that hung from their belts. Their saddle-bags were neatly loaded and their saddles had special slots for surveying equipment and coils of rope and water bottles. Sal shook her head. "They're seriously serious. We're making a big mistake."

"Why are we?" asked Humphrey.

Next to leave was Sir Montague Basingstoke-Black and his Mountaineers. The waiting crowd buzzed in excitement as they heard a distant *clip-clop, clip-clop* and the buzz became a roar as the team came into view. Mechanical horses! And not just one or two mechanical horses, but twelve pairs. Their bodies were red with gold trim and they had blue manes and tails that fluttered like flags. As they trotted onto the bridge, every knee rose and fell in unison, even though they were carrying towering loads. Humph squealed, but Sal groaned. What chance did they have against perfect beasts that didn't need to eat and would never get tired?

Beckett, who was mysteriously wearing a scarf tied over his mouth and nose, was unimpressed. "Just look at them. Top heavy. I heard they've got a table and chairs, and a folding boat, and I don't know what all."

One horse of each pair had a smaller load so there was room for a rider. Monty's twelve Mountaineers wore tweed jackets with leather elbow patches, and deerstalker hats. They still had their pipes gripped between their teeth, and now they also had rifles slung across their backs. Sir Monty rode at the front, waving and kissing his hand to the crowd. Trotting beside his horse was an elegant Belgian tracking hound.

Humphrey stood on the bench to see better. "One day I'll have a dog. Actually, a whole pack of dogs. And they'll all come when I whistle."

"Can you whistle then, Humphrey?" asked Beckett.

Humph sighed. "Not yet, silly. When I'm seven."

Sal nibbled on her thumbnail, though there wasn't much of it left to get her teeth into. "We shouldn't be doing this. Ma's going to be furious."

"No she won't," said Joe. "You're the one that gets furious, not Ma. This is going to be good. We can do it!"

She biffed him but didn't feel any better.

Monty's Mountaineers were followed by Agatha Amersham and the three other members of the Association of Women Explorers. Today they were wearing calf-length culottes with brightly striped woollen stockings, colourful jerseys and practical leather hats, and they each carried a large rucksack and a stout stick. Agatha led a pack-horse and the others marched behind swinging their arms. The nails on their boots rang out on the cobbled roadway.

"Hobnails. Good idea," said Sal.

"Why?" asked Humphrey.

"Grip," said Sal.

Next came the six Solemn men. They didn't have horses, just a regular rucksack each and a heavy-looking bundle in their arms. They stopped on the bridge and put their bundles down, then took what looked like white handkerchiefs from their pockets. They opened them out—they were bags, like large pillowcases. They dropped something into each one and almost immediately the bags started to puff up, as if downy feathers were multiplying inside. Not just feathers, but living birds, for as they grew fatter the giant pillows lifted into the air. If the men hadn't closed the ends and clipped cords to them they would have floated away like clouds. They fastened the other ends of the cords to their bundles, and the bundles rose up to knee height, then waist height, then shoulder height, and the ice axes, crampons and billycans that were hanging off them clattered into the air too.

Sal and Joe clapped. They had often discussed the possibility of such magical clouds when the straps of their rucksacks were pulling on their shoulders, but never imagined they might actually exist. All around people were exclaiming and calling out:

"Want to fetch my new stove home for me?"

"I need a couple of those to carry my old man from the beer house!"

The scientists exchanged small smirky smiles and pretended to take no notice. Then they jogged away, each with a puffy white cloud floating above them, and their bundles following behind like obedient dogs.

"That's travelling light," Sal said. "We really haven't got a chance."

Someone reported that Roger's Ruffians were still eating breakfast, so it was the Santander team's turn to cross the bridge. They all squashed onto the front seat of the dray.

"Right. Let's go, Plodder." Sal clenched her teeth; she felt jittery all over.

Beckett guided Plodder out towards the bridge. The crowd's admiring chatter about magic clouds changed into a frightening clamour.

"They're too young! Stop them!"

"Somebody rescue that dear little boy!"

Reaching hands tried to snatch Humph off the cart but he clambered over the back and ducked down out of reach between the tent and the tools. Francie whimpered and ducked down, too, her hands over her ears.

The mayor grabbed Plodder's bridle. "Oh, no you don't. Children can't take part in this."

The chairman of the Railway Company kept repeating, "I don't allow it. I certainly don't allow it!"

And the mayor's sour-faced assistant folded his arms and said, "Well, it's not my fault, I did try to tell you."

Sal had to do something. She stood up in the dray, glared at the mayor and ordered him to let go, in her most imperious voice. "I have studied the rules and there is nothing to stop us competing. Please inform our mother Angelica Santander that she can catch us up, or we will meet her on the other side of the mountains in New Coalhaven."

The grown-ups backed away. They were still tsking and tutting and shaking their heads, but they moved off the road as Beckett shook the reins and Plodder led the Santander team across the bridge.

Joe yelled, "Hooray! Go, Sal!"

As soon as they'd rounded the corner out of sight, Sal called to Beckett to stop.

"Whoops. Forgot to set the altimeter."

With shaking hands, she clamped the altimeter wheel's shank to the back of the cart. When Plodder walked on, the wheel clicked every turn in a satisfying way. The box above the wheel held the special barometric device that Angelica and Leopold Santander had invented. After every 100 clicks, a mechanical pen made a dot on the scroll of paper that wound round inside the box, and the line of dots showed the gradient of their journey. At the end of each day, Sal would join the dots to show how long their route was and how much it went up and down.

"Well remembered," said Joe. He wasn't being sarcastic.

"I shouldn't have forgotten that," she muttered. "It's probably an omen."

"We're on our way! Are you ready for adventure, young Humphrey?" said Beckett, taking off the scarf.

"Adventure!" Humphrey climbed back to the driver's bench. "All of me is excited. Even my hair."

*

They came to a fork in the road and Humphrey pointed out a drift of dust in the distance from the other teams' horses. It hung above the road to the north, directly towards the mountains.

"Good noticing, Humph," said Beckett, and guided Plodder towards the other road that ran to the west. "This is the way to my village where the donkeys live."

Joe tied a silk marker to a tree so their mother could see which way they'd gone, then walked alongside Plodder, who was living up to his name.

"I wonder why the others are all going that way?" He walked back a few paces to watch the last evidence of the other teams disappearing. "The mountains go for miles and no sensible explorer would go straight in by the first valley."

Beckett was smiling.

"Beckett?"

"What happened was, I was in the Grand Hotel last night, earning a few coins clearing tables. Most of the other teams were in the bar, boasting and bragging. The ticket man was taking bets on who'd be first, who last, who'd have the best maps and all that. I heard Sir Monty say, 'Those kiddies will never make it. What do they know about route finding?' And he laid down a sov that you'll be back inside a week."

"A sov?" Joe was shocked. "He bet a whole sovereign that we'd turn back?"

"A whole sovereign. And that's not all. Cody Cole's lot were on the whisky, and Cody sauntered up and said, 'What odds do you give me that those Santander kids will never be seen again?'"

"No!"

"He laid down five sovs against you being seen on either side of the mountains before the autumn equinox."

"That's horrible!" said Sal. "And outrageous."

"Well, that's what I thought too, so I made a plan. First, I whispered to Sir Monty's route-finder that Cody's Cowboys have already surveyed the beginning of the route, and they're definitely starting up the Prospect Valley. And I told the Cowboys' route-finder in the greatest secrecy that the Solemn men have made a scientific decision that the Prospect's the best way in."

"You didn't!" Joe exchanged astonished looks with Sal.

"The Solemn team weren't doing any betting; they were drinking energy tea and telling themselves that science can beat the world. But when one of them deliberately stuck his boot out, tripping up the serving woman and making her drop her tray, just to make his mates laugh, I decided they were as bad as the rest of them. So I told them that Sir Monty had fixed on the Prospect Valley."

"But how did you make them all believe you?" asked Sal.

Beckett looked a little embarrassed. "I just told each of them that I've wagered all I have on them winning. I told them I'd overheard something that might help."

They looked at him.

"You tricked them?" Sal sounded both shocked and impressed.

Beckett protested. "Joe, would you believe a total stranger— who's not even an adult—if they told you which route to take?"

"Course not! If they went that way without checking, they're crazy. So that's why the scarf round your face."

"I thought it'd be better if no one recognised me."

"What about Roger's Ruffians and the Agathas?" asked Sal.

"Roger's lot were all snoring away in the corner, surrounded by empty bottles. I didn't say a word to them. Nor to the women, on account of I didn't see them."

Joe couldn't stop smiling. Beckett was going to be a great asset to the Santander team; he had skills that they hadn't even known they needed. And they'd started the race!

As they went along, the altimeter clicked with every turn of the wheel, each turn registered by a counter. Every few minutes Humph ran along beside it and called out the numbers.

"We've gone 4-5-1-1 clicks."

Then after a few minutes, "It says 4-9-9-9 and it's turning to 5-0-0-0 … Now!"

So far it showed that the gradient was smooth and gradual—perfect for a railway.

CHAPTER FIVE

THE TRUTH
ABOUT FRANCIE

For many hours there was nothing to see but trees. Francie and Joe sat on the back of the dray, swinging their legs as they were bounced along by Plodder. They watched the lines of golden light cutting through the dark shadows of the branches. The stripes of sunshine would be perfect for tigers to hide in, also for wildcats and maybe leopards and ring-tailed lemurs, like the pictures in *Wonderful Wild Animals of the World*. They looked at each other and Joe knew that Francie was as happy as he was.

Mountain View Rise

They came to a clearing at the top of a rise and the view opened up for miles over the top of the forest. In the distance was a wall of misty greeny-grey mountains, and behind that floated a cigar of white cloud, and above the cloud, a line of shining white peaks gleamed against the brilliance of the sky.

Joe looked where Francie pointed and called out, "Look! Snow. That's where we're going."

"Where?" shouted Humphrey.

"Snow, though, go, woe," Carrot recited from her perch on top of the altimeter.

Beckett whistled. "You serious?"

"Real mountains!" said Sal. "I think we'd better stop here for a while. You ready, Francie?"

Francie nodded and climbed onto the top of the tent canvas to get the best view. She arranged herself cross-legged with the drawing board on her knees. She drew a wide, thin panorama, like the ones sailors have on their charts to help them recognise where they are when they come to an unfamiliar coast. She put in all the layers of hills and mountains, like an eye squinting

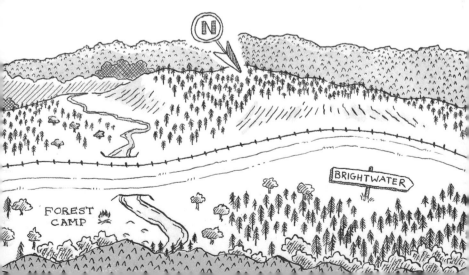

across the crumples on a bedspread. Then she put the drawing
board down. She hummed to herself as she arranged her sleeping
bag into a nest at the back of the cart, lay down, made herself
comfortable and prepared to fly …

Up and up. Above Humphrey and Beckett throwing rocks into
the stream, above Plodder grazing. Above Sal peering through
her theodolite, and Joe looking in the picnic basket. Up and up,
until the road's just a string stretched across a tweedy blanket of
summer oak, suswatch silver and darkest pine green.

Up.

Up into blissful silence. All around, the patterns of the land
spreading out—secret patterns that only birds and clouds know.

Far away: the glinting light of the River Prospect flows
towards the ocean. The river's a giant tree that grows out of the
sea instead of the soil. Its trunk passes through the hazy smudge
that is the town and across farmland and the forested plain, then
its branches fan out and climb through the hills. Beyond the
branches, smaller branches, then twigs, dividing and dividing,
higher and further, further and higher into the mountains.

One, two, three columns of dust racing alongside the trunk
of the river, towards the lower branches. Three other teams—no
sign of the fourth or fifth.

Slowly around to look west into the glare of the sun. There.
The bright gleam of another big river tree, far to the west, where
the thread of road ends at a village. The river's long and straight

and cuts right through the crumple of hills and leads deep into the heart of mountains. Its branches stretch off towards peaks that are glistening white.

Snow—the dazzling, fiery whiteness that's colder than a winter stream. One day soon.

Francie sat up slowly. Joe passed her some water and a cheese tart. She always felt tired and a bit sad when she'd been flying and food helped her feel better. He'd pinned fresh paper to her drawing board and now he watched her draw. It was a map of the panoramic view she'd drawn before she flew. It showed the town of Grand Prospect and the River Prospect stretching from the mountains to the sea, and the road through the forest that they were travelling on. And it showed the road ending at another big river, a river that flowed right into the mountains. When it was finished, she put the board aside, curled up and fell asleep.

As they were preparing to set off again, Beckett beckoned to Joe. "Can I have a quiet word?"

Joe swung himself up onto the driver's bench.

Beckett looked embarrassed and spoke quietly. "Look, I'll still try and get the donkeys like I said, but maybe I'll not come with you after all. No offence."

"What? Why?"

Beckett shuffled awkwardly. "It's just …" He glanced over his shoulder.

Joe was puzzled. "*Francie?*"

"She was lying there staring with her eyes open. I saw. Like she was possessed or something." The words tumbled out of Beckett.

He was frightened of Francie! Joe reached for her drawings. "I'll show you what she was doing." He unrolled the panorama, showing all the peaks and ridges right across the horizon.

Beckett stared. "I don't believe it," he said. "Francie drew that?"

"And this." Joe passed him the drawing board with Francie's bird's-eye view of the land, and Beckett's mouth hung open like a trout on a hook.

"That's what she was doing. Seeing from above. Seeing and putting everything she sees into her memory. Every team has someone who draws the maps. Francie's our drawer, and she's our secret weapon. She's why we've got a chance to win this race."

Beckett's mouth was still opening and closing like a dehydrating fish. Joe nudged him.

"She doesn't talk but she's the best artist in the country, probably. I bet you anything you like that everything is in the exact right place."

"But how—?"

Joe tried to explain, though he wasn't exactly sure himself.

"She flies. Not actually, because her body's still lying there. But her brain can see the landscape from above, somehow. And her eyesight's brilliant—she can zoom in like an eagle, so she can see right into the hazy distance."

"And then she draws it perfectly," Beckett shook his head. "I'd never have guessed. She looked like a scared baby when we were setting off."

Joe thought. How to explain? He opened his compass. "See the needle? It's very wobbly. Much wobblier than my old compass. That's because it's more sensitive, more accurate. Francie's like that. She experiences things *more* than other people."

"What sort of things?"

"Well, voices, say. She can hear more voices, all loud at once, which is why crowds of people are scary. All the voices make a painful racket in her head. But on the good side, colours are much brighter and she sees the shapes and patterns of everything, and she can remember them exactly, which helps her to draw."

"Does she never talk?"

"No. She draws instead. But at home, she's just normal. I mean, she can pour a cup of tea or peg out the washing—though she'll probably arrange it like a rainbow."

"Amazing." Beckett glanced down at the map again. "Truly amazing. How old is she?"

"We're eleven. How old are you?"

"Just turned fifteen."

"Sal's fourteen. She's the maths genius. She's our surveyor—our calculator."

Beckett looked startled. "Maths genius?"

"When you make a map you have to work out distances and gradients, and how high the peaks are and all that. For the railway, we need to show a route that isn't too steep for trains. Unless it's the sort of slope they can climb, of course. She can do that. She likes calculating. When she can't get to sleep she lies there working out prime numbers, and fifty decimal places of pi."

"Well, topple me with a turnip!" Beckett looked behind him. Francie was curled up between the tent poles and the water barrel, and Sal was sitting at the back of the cart squinting through Pa's uniscope. "What about you and young Humphrey, then?"

Humph was galloping ahead of the dray, waving a stick and arguing with himself. He was being a horse, the kind of talking horse that holds a sword in its front hooves.

"So far Humph's only different in an ordinary way. And I don't have any special talents. My job in the family is to find the route. Pa was teaching me. I'm going to be a route-finder like him. It's an important job in a team, but anyone can learn to do it. And I don't know anything about donkeys. None of us does. So we really need you to come with us."

Carrot swooped down onto Beckett's shoulder and rubbed her back against his cheek.

"Right." Beckett stroked Carrot. "I suppose I just never realised how many different sorts of people there are in the world." He looked at the map again and pointed to the second big river. That must be the River Brightwater. That's where my village is."

"Couldn't be better! That's the valley that Francie thinks is the best route into the mountains."

"It's the obvious way to go," said Beckett, looking pleased.

"And you'll come with us?"

"I reckon I will."

That night they stopped by a small stream just before it got dark. Francie and Joe took charge of the meal. They unpacked everything they'd saved from the feast and separated out the food that needed eating most urgently. This meant stale fishpaste sandwiches and cold vegetable fritters for dinner, squashed, but delicious. They didn't bother with a fire, so when it got dark there was nothing to compete with the stars. Joe lay back and searched the sky until he found the Great Fish constellation with its dorsal fin. This pointed north, the direction they needed to go. Maybe somewhere Ma was watching it, too, and Pa.

The moon rose between the trees, a brand new sliver of silver.

"We need to get all the way to New Coalhaven before the moon gets that small again," said Sal.

"We should wish on it," said Joe. "I wish Pa would come back."

"My father's dead," said Beckett into the darkness. "He got the coughing disease last winter. I just wish that we win, and make the railway come this way."

"I wish and wish and wish that Ma catches us up," said Sal.

Joe lit a candle so Francie could draw her wish. She wanted to touch snow.

"Snow. Me too," said Humphrey. "But also, I wish someone would tell me a story."

"I will," Joe said. He wriggled down in his sleeping bag and Humph snuggled in close. "This is the story of how Pa became an explorer."

"Good one!" said Humphrey.

"One day, Pa's mother and father took him on a visit to his grandparents' farm and he saw mountains for the very first time. The mountains above the farm were so high that there was snow on top of them, even though it was summer. One morning Pa decided he needed to touch that snow, so after breakfast he set off up the hill. At first, this meant he was on a path."

"Pa on a pa-th!" said Humphrey.

"Ha-ha. As he went up and up, his grandparents' farm got smaller and smaller down below. Grandma's aprons on the washing line became a string of colourful beads, and the cows and the pigs just spots on the green paddock.

"The path stopped at the trees and Pa climbed on up through the silent forest. He was out of breath and his legs were tired because he wasn't used to climbing in those days, but he kept going up. He came out of the trees at last but he still hadn't reached the snow. He was on a great slope of rocks that he had to scramble over. He could see the snow above him and he hoped it wasn't much further because this side of the valley was in shade, which meant it was already afternoon.

"By now he was very thirsty. He kept climbing over the rocks, and the slope got steeper, but at last he was there, at the snow. Except it wasn't like a patch of snow that he could make a snowman with, it was the end of a glacier. There was a cave under the glacier, a huge, chilly cave, like a church. Its roof was so high that Pa could stand up, and it came down into pointy icicles. Pa was really thirsty so he broke off an icicle and sucked on it, then he turned around. And he saw the world. He was higher than all the hills and the mountains around. It was like being a bird. The ridges went from dark purple to palest pink as they rose one behind another, behind another. It was the most beautiful thing he'd ever seen. And beyond the last ridge he saw the ocean for the first time. It was shining golden in the setting sun."

Humphrey wriggled round and put his head on Joe's stomach. "What about Pa's dinner?"

"He was starving. He hadn't eaten since breakfast, and now he realised how late it was. His family would be worried and it would be dark long before he got home. He looked down but the farm had vanished into the deep shadows of the valley.

"He pulled his shirtsleeve over his hand so he could hold the icicle without freezing his fingers, and set off back down the mountain. He climbed over the rocks. Then he entered the forest and it was very dark, almost too dark to see. He stumbled and fell, and scraped his knees, but he got up and carried on. He scratched his arms and legs as he felt his way down through the trees. Down, always down."

Humphrey sat up. "What about the icicle?"

"He finished it. Anyway, he started to have a strange feeling, as if someone or something was following him. A twig cracked. He called out—is someone there? But there was no answer. He stood still and listened. Sometimes he thought he could hear breathing, but he told himself he was being silly and it was just the wind in the branches. He stumbled on blindly, just with the sense that he was going downwards.

"Then suddenly, something warm and heavy hurled itself at him, knocking him down. Something was growling above him. He was terrified; his heart thumped so hard he couldn't even squeak.

"The growling stopped. Nothing had sunk its teeth into him, so he sat up, and there was a large dog sitting next to him, panting quietly. And, faintly, by the light of the stars, he could see there were no trees in front of him. The ground dropped away in a vertical cliff. The dog had appeared from nowhere to save his life."

"The wolf," Humphrey whispered.

"Pa crawled up the slope a little, away from the edge, then he sat, shivering and shaking. The dog breathed on him, warm breath, and lay down beside him so he felt the warmth of its body. When he'd recovered from the shock, Pa stood up and thanked the dog. The dog stood beside him and Pa put his hand on its shoulder, and it led the way safely down. By the time they reached the path through the fields above the farm, the moon was up. Pa saw that the dog's thick coat was silvery as the moonlight; its ears were sharp and its eyes glinted silver in the dark. Pa set off down the path, but the dog stayed at the edge of the trees. The first time Pa looked back the dog was watching him, but the second time he looked, the dog had gone. There were lights moving down below; Pa's parents and grandparents were out with lanterns looking for him. They were pretty relieved to see him, I can tell you.

"When he told them about the dog they were astonished. They asked what it looked like and he told them about its warm breath and its thick silver coat, its sharp ears and its glinting eyes.

"'That was no dog,' said Pa's grandpa. 'That was the silver wolf that saved your life. It's lived in the mountains up there for hundreds of years. No one has seen it in my lifetime, though plenty have looked for it. It's said that if you see the silver wolf you will get your heart's desire.' And they asked Pa what his heart's desire was, and they expected him to say he wanted to be rich, but he said, 'I want to be an explorer. I'm going to climb mountains and look down from the top. I want to see more of that beautiful world I saw today.' And that's what he did."

Humph took his thumb out of his mouth. "And the wolf howled, don't forget."

"Oh, yes. When Pa said that, there came a great howl, which echoed round the valley, as if the wolf was agreeing with him."

"I want to see more of the world," said Humph.

"You will. Sleep now. Twenty-six days to go," said Joe.

CHAPTER SIX

DUMPLING AND TREACLE

They reached Beckett's village in the middle of the afternoon. Joe had never seen such a sad place. Most of the buildings were deserted and their roofs had fallen in. Beckett said that the people who used to live in them had given up and moved to Grand Prospect because it was too hard to make a living so far from anywhere. Weeds grew up around the door of the smithy,

and the paddocks along the riverbank had been abandoned to thistles. The inn looked solid enough, but the roof of Beckett's cottage was covered in patches.

Beckett's mother ran to meet him with his five younger brothers and sisters. They all exclaimed and hugged. He gave his mother the coins he'd saved by doing odd jobs in Grand Prospect, and some soap and cooking oil he'd brought for her, and she hugged him again, and told him he'd grown and how his voice sounded all manly, which made his ears turn crimson.

Beckett introduced everyone, then he asked his brothers and sisters to look after Plodder.

"We're going to have a talk with Mr Arbuckle."

Mr Arbuckle was the village baker, and also the innkeeper and the ferryman who rowed hunters across the Brightwater River. There was no one in the inn, and there was nothing in the bakehouse but flies. They found him out the back, splitting logs, his face scarlet and sweat dripping off the end of his bulgy nose. When Beckett asked him to lend his donkeys, he just snorted.

"We'll pay you double," Sal offered recklessly. "Double whatever the rate is for donkeys, when we return them."

Mr Arbuckle pulled out a hanky and mopped his neck. "You won't return," he said. "Few people have crossed those *bare steeps where desolation stalks.*"

"Stalks," said Carrot, eyeing him from a log.

"Shh!" Sal was sucking on the end of her plait—a sure sign that she was anxious. But Beckett didn't look bothered; he gently persuaded Mr Arbuckle to rest in the shade of a tree, and he squatted in front of him.

"Mr Arbuckle, sir. You are the leader of this village and a wise man. This competition is to find a way through the mountains between Grand Prospect and New Coalhaven, so folks can get to New Coalhaven more easily. First, just a horse track, but then—a railway! Now, I want you to imagine something ..."

Beckett spoke in a way that made everyone want to listen. Mr Arbuckle leaned back against the tree trunk and fanned himself with his hat.

"Sir, I want you to imagine that the winning route comes through this village. First, surveyors pass through here, and engineers. They stay in your inn. Next up, the railway builders arrive. They need to be fed and watered. Then trains come through. Everyone buys your famous pies. You get your *Daily Bugle* on the day it's printed, instead of a week late. You grow rich." He paused. Mr Arbuckle was listening closely. "You can afford to pay someone to cut your firewood. Your back stops hurting. The village grows. We become somewhere. We need a mayor—" He paused dramatically. "We elect you, Mr Arbuckle!"

Joe was impressed. Beckett had thought a lot about what having a railway station would mean to his village, and Mr Arbuckle seemed to believe every word—for a minute. Then he noticed Humph, who was trying to do a somersault, bottom up and one leg waving in the air, and he became cross. "That's ridiculous. How do you imagine that you children could ever win? I've read about this competition in the *Daily Bugle*. There's a team of scientists who've entered. And Sir Monty Whatsit—he's famous. And Cody Cole, that professional explorer. And you think you lot can beat them? Ridiculous."

But Beckett hadn't finished. "Sir, they may not be fully grown, but the Santanders have been trained by their famous explorer parents, and they all have special skills. The competition is to produce a route and also to make a map. Like this."

He smoothed out Francie's map. Mr Arbuckle glanced at it, then he peered more closely. There was silence, then he let out his breath in a long whistle.

"Who drew this? When?" He looked at them all in turn.

"Francie drew this yesterday, sir," said Sal.

"Extraordinary." He looked at Francie, who was busy sketching him, and at Joe and Sal, sitting cross-legged on the ground. "Quite extra-ordinary." His finger traced the road between Grand Prospect and the village.

Then Francie did something she'd never done before. She carefully tore out the page she'd been working on and held it out for Mr Arbuckle to take. It was a terrific portrait, just how he must have looked about twenty years before, but with a normal-shaped nose.

55

He blinked. "I say." He swallowed. "I say, I say!" He fanned his face with his hat. "My goodness, what a likeness." He hesitated, his voice uncertain, almost apologetic. "But I need my donkeys. I use them every day."

Beckett had the answer for everything. "We will leave you our horse and dray to use while we're away, sir. It's a fair exchange and I promise you won't regret it."

That night they stretched out in a row under the apricot tree in Beckett's garden. As soon as Humph was asleep, Joe called out quietly, "Beckett! Beckett? Who does Plodder actually belong to?"

Beckett cleared his throat. "Um ... I've no idea."

"What?" Joe and Sal exclaimed together.

"Well I hadn't eaten in ages. I was watching the preparations in the square and wondering how to lay my hands on a loaf of bread, when this man asks can I drive a horse and dray? I says, course I can, since I was knee-high, and he says, take this horse to the station to meet the last expedition and there's a free feed for you. The driver had got into a fight and his nose was pouring blood. But the bleeding man was just the driver. Plodder wasn't his horse. I've no idea who owns him. I just picked you up and took you to the town square and now here we are."

"D'you mean we've *stolen* him?" asked Sal.

"Borrowed," said Joe, "because we really, really needed the donkeys. Twenty-five days to go."

*

Dumpling was a honey-coloured female and Treacle was a black male donkey. They were fully grown but seemed very small. The Santanders looked at the mountain of equipment and essential supplies they'd unloaded from the dray, and at the four harvesting baskets Beckett had borrowed from his mother, which the donkeys would carry as panniers.

They started to make piles. Ma's clothes, her darning bag, and the lesson books she used to teach them latin, history and astronomy were easy choices for the "leave" pile, but everything else seemed equally essential.

"So now what?" said Joe. The "take" pile was still a ten-donkey load.

"What now?" said Carrot.

Beckett laughed and picked up *Simpson's Grammar Explained*. "Did you teach that bird to talk?"

Joe held out a piece of unripe apricot to Carrot. "Ma rescued her from a schoolroom. Carrot spent years listening to Miss Wilton-Clark, the world's bossiest teacher."

"I'm glad I don't ever have to go to school again." Beckett dumped the grammar with the other books on the back of the cart.

They tried packing the other way: essential stuff first, then what they still had room for. The food, the cooking pot and the billy for heating water fitted into two baskets. The surveying and map-making equipment, the groundsheets, the bucket, the axe, the slasher, the spade and Humph's rucksack filled the other two. Everything else had to be left behind. Easy.

Sal shook her head. "We need the tent. This is impossible."

Joe liked sleeping in the tent but he hated all the hammering-in of pegs and slotting together of poles at night, and wrangling the canvas back into its bag in the morning. "We'll be hours quicker without it. It's summer. We'll sleep under the stars, and we can always shelter under the tarpaulin if it rains."

"When it rains," said Sal.

It was Joe's turn to worry when Beckett sliced lengths off the coil of rope to tie the baskets together in pairs. Pa and Ma always said *carry the longest rope you can*, but there was no alternative.

Beckett's mother found some old sacks to protect the donkeys' backs; they loaded Treacle with the baskets of tools and the net of hay Mr Arbuckle gave them, and Dumpling got the food baskets. The empty water barrel was tied on top, and the altimeter rolled along behind.

Beckett's mother suggested they take the groundsheets out of Treacle's baskets and drape them over each donkey's load.

"You never know when it'll start to rain," she said, "or if you have to walk under a waterfall."

That made a tiny bit more room. Sal stuffed in Ma's first-aid bag, Joe added an extra bag of route-marking silks, Beckett rescued Pa's fishing rod from the "no" pile, and Francie held out the paraffin bottle and the lantern, which was much better for drawing in the dark than a candle. Sal managed to shove them all in with the tools.

They checked their rucksacks: a sleeping bag, a change of clothes, plus another jersey and two extra pairs of underwear and socks, a warm jacket, a woolly hat, gloves and a rain cape, a mug, a bowl, a pocket knife and a spoon, some candles and matches.

Joe also had his bag of orange silks, a ball of twine and the coil of rope. Francie carried her sketchbook, pencils, pens and ink.

Humph was wearing old shorts of Joe's and his favourite red jersey. Sal, Francie and Joe were all wearing comfy old shirts of Pa's, with the sleeves shortened. Sal had her own trousers that Ma had made her, and Joe and Francie had Pa's old trousers taken in at the waist and cut off at the knee and held up by braces (Francie) and a belt (Joe). They all had good boots that fitted—unlike Beckett's boots that flapped at the toe. His mother made him take them off while she waxed a thread and sewed them up. She gave him his father's old socks, jersey and overcoat for when it got cold, which made his eyes water a bit and he had to blow his nose.

He didn't have a rucksack of his own, so Joe emptied out Ma's for him, and gave him her sleeping bag.

"But what about when she catches us up?" Sal whispered.

"Beckett's a definite, Ma's only maybe. If she does catch us up, she'll find what she needs," said Joe. "She'll manage."

When all the belongings they were leaving behind had been stowed in one of Mr Arbuckle's empty rooms, and Beckett had his boots back on, they waved goodbye to his family and set off along the river bank, leading two heavily laden donkeys.

Humphrey could walk for hours so long as he had someone to chat to, and Beckett was a good talker so long as he had someone listening, so Humph stuck close and Beckett told him stories about the dirigible and the steam-driven charabancs he'd seen in Grand Prospect. He'd even seen a mining engine called The Worm that could burrow coal and gold out of the ground.

Francie and Joe left markers for Ma, in case she followed them. Francie arranged coloured stones in little cairns every few hundred clicks while Joe tied a strip of orange silk to a branch at eye level, so it fluttered in the sunshine.

Sal walked behind Dumpling, watching the altimeter and dodging the donkey poo. "Blooming donkeys! No need to waste your silks, Joe, the donkeys are leaving their own trail for Ma."

But the biggest problem with the donkeys was that they kept stopping to graze.

"You sure these beasts are donkeys, Beckett?" Sal tugged at Dumpling's halter, but Dumpling just reached for another mouthful of thistles. "Sure we're not trying to drag two tortoises over the mountains?"

Joe pushed Treacle's rump. "Come on, you! This isn't a snail race."

Treacle just flicked his tail in Joe's face and put his nose into a wild rose bush.

It was Carrot who got them moving. She flew down and perched between Dumpling's ears and screeched: "Sit straight, face front!"

Like magic, Dumpling started moving, and Treacle followed. And they kept going, as long as Carrot snapped at them from time to time.

To begin with there was hardly any need for route finding—the way was directly up the wide, straight valley of the Brightwater River. When they came to a fork in the river,

Joe checked his compass and Francie's sketch map and decided which branch of the river to take. The ground was level, the rise was gentle, and there was plenty of room for a railway track.

The river sparkled and they wanted to jump in. It was a baking hot afternoon but Sal kept hurrying them along the river bank where there wasn't much shade. The shadows grew longer and longer until finally Beckett said the donkeys had to stop, even if the Santanders didn't. At last. They pulled their boots off and threw themselves into the cool water. Beckett couldn't swim, but he sat in the shallows and let Humph splash him.

In the middle of the night Humph cried out that he wanted Ma, and he sobbed and sobbed. Joe cuddled him and whispered, "You'll see her soon. Just think, this is our second night on the race already. Only twenty-four days to go."

CHAPTER SEVEN

A TRUE
LIFE BEAR!

In the morning Humphrey could hardly open his eyes. His whole face was swollen and his skin was stretched and shiny as a currant bun. After swimming, everyone had rubbed themselves with citronella against the stoneflies, but no one had helped poor Humph. Sal gave him a sugar biscuit so he knew how sorry they all were, then they had to unpack Treacle's baskets to find Ma's pot of salve to smear over the swollen welts on his face and arms. He was brave, but tears kept trickling down his puffy cheeks.

Sal made porridge for breakfast and it was just as burnt and lumpy as it had been every morning so far, but there was plenty of sugar so they managed to eat it. No one wanted to scrub out the pot, though, so they left the burnt bits on. They'd meant to start early, but the sun was quite high before they set off again.

"Why are we trying to do this without Ma?" Sal muttered to Joe as they squelched through a boggy place. "We shouldn't be doing our first race on our own. It isn't just about finding a route and making the maps, you know."

"What else, then? We just have to keep going and get there."

"What about meals? Insect bites? And I don't know what else until it happens, that's the whole problem." Sal's voice rose to a despairing squeak.

"We'll be all right," he said. "Stop worrying. We'll be fine."

She glared at him. "Stop saying that, Joseph Santander. This was your idea but you're leaving all the worrying up to me. Which is just not fair. You keep saying 'we'll be fine' all the time. *But what if we're not?*"

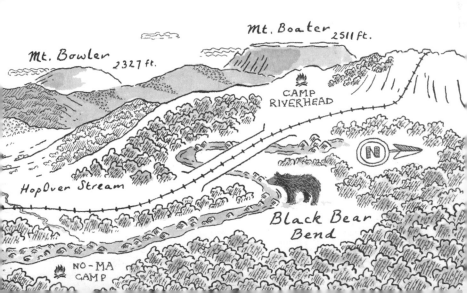

Luckily for Joe, who didn't really have an answer, the measuring wheel's bell dinged to show a thousand clicks and Sal stopped shouting at him and concentrated on calculating heights and distances and angles instead. She wrote down the answers on a rough sketch map.

Every time they stopped, Francie's pencil danced. She drew the landscape to remind herself what needed to go on the map: two long scrolls on spare altimeter paper, one showing the west, and one the east side of the valley, her drawings growing at lightning speed as they moved along the river bank. If someone had fallen from a cloud into that long valley they could have unrolled her pictures, looked around, and pointed to exactly where they were. There was the big slip, like a scar on the cheek of the hillside. There was the enormous tree that lay across the river like a sieve, collecting stones and bones and bare-branched bushes.

They agreed that they'd take it in turns to name things, so Beckett named the shining thread of a waterfall that they saw in the distance "Phoebe Falls" after his little sister.

"Which do you think sounds better?" said Joe, hurling a stone that landed in the river with a satisfying splosh. "Lake Joseph or Mount Joseph? Or maybe the River Joe? That would be good, if it was a really big river."

"Joseph's Creek?" suggested Sal.

"Joseph Santander Pond?" said Beckett.

"Joe's puddle!" said Humphrey.

Joe laughed. "Humphrey's piddle more like!"

*

As they went upstream there was less and less water in the river, until it was just several sun-flecked trickles, each finding its own way through the shingle riverbed. There was plenty of space for the donkeys, and whenever the other side looked easier to walk along, they just splashed across. Here and there, whole dead trees lay around on the stones. Sal tried to imagine the river big enough and fast enough to shift huge trees. It was easier to imagine giants throwing them around.

They were keeping to the shade in the hot afternoon when Francie pulled at Sal's shirt and pointed behind them. She gave Sal the uniscope.

Trees, trees, trees. Then … something moving. Something white. A long way down the valley.

"Oh, please let that be Ma." Sal sucked on the end of her plait.

Joe stopped and peered back, too. "Ma's got a white shirt, hasn't she, Francie?"

Francie nodded. It could be Ma, it really could.

Sal thought she heard a shout. She kept looking back, but there was no sign of the white whatever-it-was. She tried to remind herself that Ma had no way of getting to Grand Prospect, but she couldn't help going slower anyway, just in case, and she insisted they stop for the night much earlier than they had the night before. After they'd eaten, she suggested they sing some songs, because she secretly hoped that Ma would follow the noise and appear through the trees. But Ma didn't, and eventually Sal decided they'd better save their breath for walking.

Joe yawned. "Twenty-three days to go."

*

The next day walking became harder, and so did drawing, as the trees grew so thickly they blocked the view. The valley sides were closer and steeper and Sal had to steer the altimeter around boulders, and up and down banks. Sometimes Joe made a zigzag path around a steep place that the railway track could cut through.

They kept looking back and listening. Finally, Francie saw something move behind them. She drew a horse.

"Another team?" said Joe.

"It could still be Ma," said Sal. "She could have borrowed a horse. You can check next time you fly, Francie."

Next time. Flying was too exhausting to do often.

In the afternoon, the valley opened out again. Invisible birds called in the trees, hawks floated high above them, and swifts and flycatchers darted above the water. Humphrey fought against the quiet by singing loudly.

> *Chocolate or apple cake*
> *Fruit cake or nut*
> *We can eat any cake*
> *That our Ma can bake*
> *Just take a knife and*
> *Cut us a slice of*
> *Chocolate or apple cake*

Sal tried to ignore him, but Beckett soon got fed up with that song and taught him a new one.

A bear he went fishing all down in the stream
Hey ho, to catch him a fish
He stood by the water as if in a dream
Hey ho, to catch him a fish
He saw a fat trout and in went his paw
Hey ho, to catch him a fish
Out came the trout all hooked on his claw
Hey ho, he'd caught him a fish

Joe and Sal joined in and they were all singing loudly when Beckett stopped, held out his arm and hissed, "Shh! Don't move! Do we have any weapons?"

Sal laughed but Beckett's face was serious. He put his finger to his lips and then pointed at a rock at the edge of the water. Except it wasn't a rock. It was a huge black bear, and it sat up and looked straight at them. It was as if the song had magic powers.

Beckett held tight to Treacle's halter and Sal hung on to Dumpling. She felt in Dumpling's basket without taking her eyes off the bear, which was glaring at them, unmoving. She was feeling for the kitchen knife but found only the lid of the cooking pot, more shield than weapon.

The bear pushed up onto four paws and padded a few steps in their direction. Joe scooped up some stones; Sal pushed Humph behind her and brandished the lid.

Dumpling danced sideways.

The bear took a short run towards them.

Joe yelped and Francie and Sal moved close to Joe and pulled the donkeys into the huddle. The bear paused.

It was just a few yards away. It reared up on its hind legs—a great wall of powerful blackness. It stared at them as if it was deciding where to start, then it opened its mouth and snarled, its long canines shiny with drool. Joe's stones bounced off its fur.

Dumpling and Treacle kicked and snorted. Someone shrieked. The blade of Beckett's pocketknife flashed. Sal clanged the lid against the spade.

The bear dropped to all fours and started towards them, growling. Sal could smell the foul fishy scent of its breath and see its muscles rippling as it tensed to pounce.

Then Dumpling let out a blood-curdling scream.

The bear came to a dead stop in a flurry of shingle and rose up onto its hind legs again. It towered over them, claws slashing the air, teeth ready to crunch down on bone. Its eyes rolled white as the unearthly screech came again, bouncing off the valley walls. It was louder than a steam engine's whistle, as loud as thunder right overhead.

The bear threw itself sideways and ran. It crashed through the bushes and vanished into the trees, away from Dumpling.

Sal's legs crumpled. She sat down; her insides felt like water.

Joe dropped down beside her. "It would have killed us. Ripped us to shreds."

"Those teeth."

"And those claws!"

Humph had been squashed behind the others, so he hadn't seen the bear when it ran towards them and didn't quite realise how much danger they'd been in. He bounced up and down with excitement. "D'you see that? It was a bear! In true life!

A true life bear! Did you see it, Sal? Did you see the bear, Francie?"

Francie stared after the bear, then started to draw it running, its fur rippling.

The lid clattered out of Sal's trembling fingers. "It was that close! Has it gone? Really gone?"

"Stupid, stupid, stupid." Beckett dug in his rucksack and pulled out a catapult. "I should have been prepared, I should always have it ready." He filled his pocket with pebbles and fitted one to the cradle.

He aimed at a white bird that was sitting on a rock, and the stone landed near enough to send it flapping into the air.

"I wasn't trying to hurt it," he reassured Humph.

Carrot refused to ride on Dumpling's head again, but it didn't matter because as soon as she'd eaten her reward apple Dumpling twitched her ears forward and set off without even being told.

They armed themselves with big sticks, which they thumped to keep time as they walked.

"That shiny stone," said Beckett, pulling back the cradle of his catapult.

"How can a pebble win against a bear?" Sal asked as the shiny stone flew into the air.

Beckett aimed at a rock in the river. "Hit it on the nose, or in the eye, it'll run away quick enough."

That evening they reached the head of the valley. The slope all round was so steep it was practically vertical, and thickly blanketed in forest.

Beckett looked around, puzzled. "So where does the train track go from here?"

"Either through a tunnel or it climbs up, depending on what's at the top," said Sal.

Francie took herself off to a quiet hollow to fly before it got dark, so she could give Joe an idea of what lay ahead. Joe wished she didn't have to fly, but she needed to see from above before she drew her maps. And if Joe didn't have her sketch map to help him decide the best way, they could waste days exploring valleys that took them in the wrong direction.

A couple of years ago, Joe had overheard a conversation in the tent in which Ma had tried to make Pa understand how exhausting flying was, and that she was afraid Francie wasn't strong enough. Pa had said, *flying is an extraordinary gift. Francie must be encouraged to fly as much as she can, so she builds up her stamina.*

But Joe worried. When Francie came back from flying her skin looked grey and it was a huge effort for her to stay awake long enough to draw what she'd seen. All he could do was make sure she slept, but he noticed that she had to sleep for longer and longer now before she was back to her normal self.

"We ought to make a big f-i-r-e because of b-e-a-r-s or w-o-l-v-e-s," Sal spelled out to Joe, over Humph's head.

Humph looked indignant. "I'm not sleepy!"

Joe laughed. "That's not what Sal was spelling! She said let's have a big fire."

As they dragged branches back to the camp, he was pleased they'd thought about being kind and not scaring Humphrey. If Humph was worried that something was waiting behind a tree he might refuse to walk and then they'd really be in trouble. Most children Humph's age weren't nearly such good walkers.

"So, what's for dinner?" asked Beckett when they'd got the fire going.

"Dinner?" Sal was re-reading the race instructions. She'd already read them at least twice and reassured them all that Francie's maps and drawings were just what the organisers wanted, but she wanted to check she was doing the right calculations.

"We've finished the leftovers and I'm not eating porridge again," said Beckett.

"Nor me," said Joe. "What else is there?"

Sal straightened up. "Porridge is the only thing I know how to cook."

"No offence, like, but porridge is one of the many things you *don't* know how to cook," said Beckett.

"Well, I'm sorry my porridge isn't up to your high standards," Sal snapped. "I'm a mathematician, not the flipping chef."

Beckett looked around slowly. "Who is the flipping chef?"

Joe scratched some burnt scrapings off the side of the porridge pot. "Ma's always done the cooking. And Pa when he was here."

"What exactly were you planning to eat on this expedition of yours?" asked Beckett.

"I don't know. Food." Sal shrugged. "I didn't really think about it."

Beckett shook his head in disbelief. Finally, he said, "I'll make dinner."

CHAPTER EIGHT

A STORY THAT ISN'T REALLY ABOUT A PIG

"What about the caterpull?" said Humph.

Beckett passed him the catapult. "Work it out." Joe hadn't heard Beckett sound grumpy before. He hurried to give him a hand.

"Stupid me. I just assumed—" Beckett's voice went squeaky then growly. "I just assumed that you lot would have the basics nailed—like cooking—since you could do the fancy stuff—like making maps. Goes to show. Even my six-year-old sister can make perfect porridge."

They laid all the food out on the groundsheet and considered it, together. Some apples, the jar of pickles and the whole cheese (a bit sweaty) left from the feast. Some carrots and potatoes, a bag each of dried peas and beans, and a jar of special bread starter from Beckett's mother. And then there were the supplies they'd brought with them on the train: a tin each of sugar biscuits and raisins, bags of flour, rice, oats, tea, a tin of lard, a flitch of bacon that smelled of smoke, and a tube of salt. And half a bag of sugar.

Joe bit into a carrot. "It looks like a lot of food."

"Not nearly enough," said Beckett. "Unless we're very, very careful."

Beckett knew how to cook. He scrubbed out the pot and chopped two carrots into it with rice, water, salt and some bits of bacon, and added some green leaves he'd picked by the stream. Then he made bread dough using some of the starter from his mother's special jar.

While they waited for dinner Joe showed Humph how to make an H for Humphrey out of sticks. Then they practised drawing A for apple, B for bear and C for Carrot in the dirt, while a yawning Francie drew a sketch map for Joe, and a picture

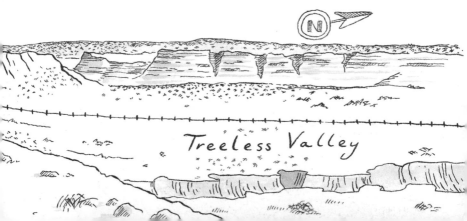

Treeless Valley

of what she'd seen. No Ma. But just a little way down the river, a white horse and at least two people.

"It has to be another team," said Joe. "But which one?"

Francie shrugged.

"Who had a white horse, Humph? Not the Cowboys or the Solemn men?"

"No. The mechanical horses weren't white."

"Maybe the women's team?"

Humph shook his head. "Their horse was brown."

"Must be Roger Rumpledown's team, then," said Joe. "And they're coming this way."

The Santanders had decided to stay where they were for two nights. It would mean Joe could go ahead by himself to explore the next part of the route, and Francie and Sal could finish the map of the journey so far. Sal broke up a long branch to feed into the fire and admitted to Joe that the real reason she'd suggested staying put was because she'd hoped Ma would catch them up.

"But that's not Ma behind us." She stamped on a branch to snap it. "And most likely she hasn't even got to Grand Prospect yet. And if there's a team right behind us, well, maybe we should all go on together?"

"How do we have the best chance of winning? Best map or first back?" asked Beckett, who was stirring the dinner pot.

"Best map," said Sal.

Joe agreed. "Francie should get as much time as possible for map work."

Beckett settled it. "Then we should definitely stay here for a day. Dumpling's got a cut on her leg. If she rests it and we bathe it tomorrow, it'll heal. If not, there's a chance it may fester."

So they tried to forget about Roger Rumpledown and concentrate on dinner instead. It tasted even better than it smelled. Joe ran his finger round the bowl to get the last drop and licked it.

"That was a miracle. I vote we make Beckett expedition chef from now on. All those in favour?"

Everyone raised their spoons.

Beckett wiped out the cooking pot and put the risen dough into it, nestled the pot in the hot embers of the fire, and shovelled more glowing embers onto the lid to bake his bread.

"Suits me," he said. "But I can't be the cook unless I'm in charge of food as well. And I make the rules about it. Actually, there's only one rule: *No helping yourselves.* Not to anything."

They all agreed. It was easy to agree with a full stomach. They banked up the fire with slow-burning suswatch branches and snuggled down in their sleeping bags close together.

But despite being exhausted, no one slept, except Francie. A twig snapped. A branch scraped. Some animal cried, far away. Something rustled through the ferns, and they all held their breath.

"Is it a bear?" Humphrey whispered.

"No, it's something very small. A mouse," said Sal. "I'll tell you a story if you promise to go to sleep after. A true story about some noises that I heard one night in our tent."

Humph wriggled close to her. "I promise."

*

"A long time ago, when I was a bit younger than you, Pa and Ma were making a map of the lakes in the western mountains. It was summer and we lived in the tent. The water was warm and Pa taught me to swim, and Ma taught me to read.

"Then one night I woke up and heard this funny *whoof-whoof-whoof* sound. The lantern was bright on the other side of the blanket that hung down to make a separate sleeping space for me, so I whispered, 'Pa, what's that?'

"And he said, 'It's all right, Sal, it's just a hedgehog snuffling around outside. I'll shoo it away. Go back to sleep.'

"So I did. And a bit later I heard a louder sound, like a *grunt, grunt, grunt*. And I called out, 'Pa, what's that?'

"And he said, 'It's all right, Sal, it's just a wild pig outside the tent. I'll shoo it away. Go back to sleep.'

"So I did. But a bit later I woke up and I could hear another noise that wasn't a snuffle or a grunt—it was a cry. 'Waaaa!'

"I sat up in bed and said, 'Pa, what's that?'

"And he said, 'It's a baby—your new baby brother.'

"A brother? Ma and Pa had me, we didn't need a baby in the family. So I said, 'Shoo it away and I'll go back to sleep.'

"But Pa said no. He carried me in to say hello to Joe, who was tiny and wrapped in a towel, lying in Ma's arms.

"And then Ma said, 'Holygamoley, Pa, there's another one coming!' And Pa put me back on my side of the curtain and tucked baby Joe in next to me.

"And that hedgehog began to whoosh again and the pig began to grunt but I hardly heard because baby Joe's face went red and all screwed up and he began to bellow: 'Wah, wah, wah.' And I said, 'Shh, baby, shh, I'm your big sister,' and then I put my knuckle against his mouth and he sucked on it, and his face went calm, and he looked at me with his big dark eyes. And I thought, maybe this brother will be all right."

"Not just all right," said Joe. "You thought, this brother is amazing!"

"Not bad," said Sal. "He wasn't bad. And by the time Pa lifted baby Joe up again he was fast asleep. Then I saw that Ma was feeding another baby and that was Francie. She'd arrived into the world without making a sound."

"And what about me? Why aren't I there?" Humph was cross.

"You weren't born yet, not for ages," said Joe.

Humph was always grumpy when he remembered they'd been a family before he was born and they shared memories that didn't include him.

"It's mean. You should have waited for me."

"We did," said Sal. "And here you are."

"Twenty-two days to go," said Joe. "Sleep time, baby Humph."

When Joe got up, it felt as if the whole world was still sleeping. The valley was filled with mist and even the dawn warblers sounded muffled. Carrot flew on to his shoulder as he started the long climb to the top of the ridge. To begin with he couldn't help thinking about bears, but there were no signs of any big animals—no scat, no bits of fur caught on a prickle bush, no paw prints—and soon he stopped thinking about wild animals and concentrated on finding a route. All through last year, Ma had set him tests: *find a way to the top of that hill; find the most direct route home*, so it wasn't the first time he'd been on his own in a strange place, but this was the first time he was exploring on his own for real; the first time it mattered that he did a good job. *No rush; take care.*

Everything was still, and damp, and smelled of earth. His feet moved silently on the thick moss that grew under the trees, although he made plenty of noise with Pa's slasher.

Swish-swash. He sliced through thorny creepers.

Smack-crack. He snapped off dead branches.

It was no use scrambling straight up; he had to make a path the donkeys could follow, and that could be widened for carts one day. So he zigged and zagged, back-tracking every time the slope became too steep, and he marked every bend in the route with a strip of orange silk. It was slow work. Carrot kept stopping to poke in the bark of branches for grubs but she always caught up again.

After a while the trees thinned until he could see where he was going, and then the sun came out, and soon after that he was above the tree line, above the shade. Sweat dribbled down his cheeks and the back of his neck burned until he took off his over-shirt and draped it over his head. He'd had a sunhat when they started but he'd lost it.

Onwards. Upwards. This was taking a very long time.

Finally, the slope levelled out.

"We did it, Carrot! We've got to the top."

"Top marks!" Carrot flew to his arm and together they looked out across a strange and unrecognisable world. The Brightwater

Valley was filled with a white ocean of mist, dotted with island peaks that stuck up above it. Sal had called the round-topped mountain "Mt Bowler" and the flat-topped one "Mt Boater".

It was a brilliant day.

Joe took out his lunch even though the sun was nowhere near overhead. Beckett had left a sandwich and an apple for him, and Joe had added a few raisins and a hunk of cheese. Beckett's bread was dense and moist, and a hundred times more delicious than the dry bricks Ma produced on the campfire.

Carrot looked hopeful.

"I'll give you some of my water. Not my sandwich, though."

The parrot rubbed her crest in the little puddle of water Joe poured into his palm and shook herself.

When he'd finished his lunch, Joe looked around. This was perfect for the Vertical. A climbing train could come straight up the incline he'd zigzagged up, and the hilltop was practically flat. Couldn't be better. Beyond, the land sloped gently down into a broad, empty valley that stretched to the north, towards the snowcapped mountains in the distance. They were a lot nearer than when Joe had first seen them from the road to Beckett's house. They'd already come a very long way.

There was no mist in this valley, and no trees, just a few patches of low bushes. Francie had drawn a rough route when she'd woken up after flying, but she couldn't tell from above what was firm and what was bog, or just how steep a slope was. It was Joe's job to find the actual path along the valley, and then up and over a long rim of hills that Francie had called Crocodile Ridge to wherever they needed to go next.

He scanned the landscape and listened. Nothing but the trickle of a tiny stream flowing under the heather, the hums of invisible insects, and a skytrill, flying too high to see. He was the only thing moving about in all that high wild land, apart from Carrot.

Be observant, Pa had said. *Watch what's growing and how it grows, feel the direction of the wind, watch the shadows, see which way the water's flowing. Use your compass and your brain. Always leave markers. And don't forget to turn around often so you know what the journey back should look like.*

Pa had always said he'd walk alongside Joe when he found his first route. Walk alongside him but let Joe make all the decisions. He was the only other person who knew what finding a route involved. But he wasn't there. Joe sang "The Song of the Mountain Builder" and tried not to think about anything except the land around him.

He walked miles that day. The route for the train had to have few ups-and-downs, no zig-zags and not too many stream crossings. The markers were a problem because there were no trees to hang them from, so he had to tie them to bushes where they weren't always easy to see. He often had to backtrack, collecting up his markers as he went, then setting off a little higher up the slope, or lower, to avoid a steep drop. He was pleased with himself, and thought if Pa had been there, he'd have said, *Well done, son, you're using your brain and remembering everything I told you. Good work.*

When the sun was showing about two o'clock, he started the long trek back to the camp, following his silks. Just before he reached the zigzag down through the trees he was startled by a loud snort. He froze, in case it was something fierce, and looked around slowly. Not a wolf, but a large white horse. Stretched out in the sun nearby and snoring softly were Roger Rumpledown and his three Ruffians. Joe sneaked past before they saw him.

How weird. In all this vast landscape, why were the Rumpledown Ruffians right by his path?

By the time he got back to camp, his legs were aching, his stomach was flapping and he felt like sleeping for a week. But he knew he'd found the best way into the broad valley and flagged a good level route halfway along it, and he hadn't got lost *and* he'd got back before dark so no one would be worried. He was looking forward to hearing the others say, "Here's Joe! Well done, Joe," or possibly, "You're brilliant! Wonderful! What an achievement."

But that's not what happened.

CHAPTER NINE

AN UNSWALLOWABLE ROCK

While Joe had been finding the next section of their route, Sal and Francie had worked on the map of the route they'd already travelled. Sal opened the altimeter and unrolled the scroll of paper inside. She was relieved to see that the altimeter was working perfectly. There were hundreds of dots along the scroll, one for every hundred clicks of the altimeter wheel, and they rose gradually up the width of the paper from the starting point

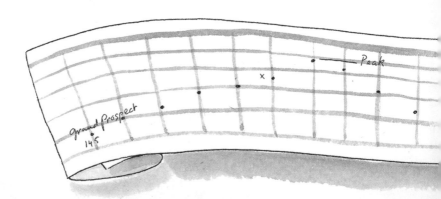

at Grand Prospect (145 feet above sea level) to this clearing at 920 feet above sea level. Less than one foot up for every one hundred feet along—perfect for trains.

She sharpened a pencil with her pocketknife and opened her notebook. She had the whole day to do what she liked doing best, which was trigonometry. How high was each peak? How far below their track was the river? What was the gradient of the slope ahead?

Time passed. When Sal finally glanced up she was astonished to see that the sun was already hidden behind the trees. How did it get to be afternoon already? And where was Humphrey?

"Have you seen the boys?"

Francie shook her head without looking up.

"Where did they go?"

Francie shrugged.

"Francie!" Sometimes Francie was exasperating.

Francie sighed, screwed the lid on her ink pot, put down the pen with which she'd been drawing tiny trees to represent the forest, and stood up. She let her eyes go squinty and turned slowly round in a circle. Her nose was up as though she were

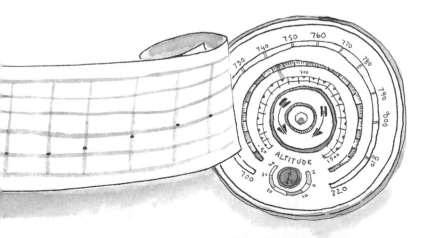

sniffing the air. At last she nodded downhill and gave Sal a look that said *nothing terrible has happened to Humphrey* and Sal had to be satisfied.

She cut them both some bread and cheese and gave the list of heights she'd made to Francie, who was adding colour wash to the map she'd drawn: very thick forests were dark green, and places that were easy to walk she coloured pale pink. All the features were neatly labelled in Francie's tiny handwriting: Black Bear Bend, Mt Beckett (2601 feet), Wait-for-Me Stream, Hop Over Stream, Crocodile Ridge and Lost Knife Gully.

"Where could they have gone?"

Francie ignored her.

Sal listened hard. Insects buzzed and hummed. A cuckoo called, and a lizard rustled away under the leaves. No voices. That morning Sal had snapped at Humph to stop asking questions and leave her in peace, but now she wished she could hear his insistent voice saying, "Sal? Hey, Sal?"

Beckett was all right. No, he was excellent at what he was good at: cooking, managing donkeys, entertaining Humph. But he wasn't an explorer. He didn't have a compass. Five steps into the forest and you could be lost forever.

She called and called, but there were no answering shouts.

How long should she give them before starting to search? What on earth were they doing anyway, going off without telling her? Anything could have happened. Bears. Snakes. And neither of them could swim. Cliffs. A broken leg was all they needed. Didn't Beckett realise they mustn't take risks—they all had to be fit and in one piece to tackle the high mountains. She was getting more and more furious inside, so when Beckett and Humphrey strolled out of the trees with the donkeys, she bellowed, "Where the hell have you been?"

Beckett looked shocked. "You knew where we were."

"How could I know?"

"You could know," Beckett said slowly, in his most annoying, patient voice, "because I told you. So did Humphrey. I said, 'We're going down to that pool we passed, to bathe the donkeys and to see if we can catch a fish.' Humph said he'd dug some worms for bait. And you answered, 'Right-o, good.'"

"Oh." Sal could have apologised then, but instead she said, "I hope you caught something."

"Well, no, we didn't."

"So what are we having for dinner?"

"You can eat boiled grass for all I care," Beckett growled.

A few minutes later there was a terrible howl from the food store. He'd found the cheese hacked into and left unwrapped, the raisin tin lighter than it had been, and, worst of all, that someone had helped themselves to the bag of sugar and left it open. A procession of ants was carrying it away, grain by grain.

"That's it," he said in an icy voice, stuffing his greatcoat into his rucksack. "You all promised, but it seems the promise of a Santander isn't worth two ears of barley. If I can't trust you, I can't travel with you, so I'm going home. Your mother can get her rucksack and sleeping bag back when you return the donkeys. If you return the donkeys."

*

When Joe walked into their camp expecting to be hailed a hero, Humphrey hurled himself at him, red-eyed and sobbing.

"Beckett's gone," he cried. "Sal shouted and Beckett's gone."

"Going, going, gone," Carrot shrieked, digging her claws into Joe's arm.

Before Joe could even open his mouth to ask what happened, Sal screamed at him to help Francie. "Quick!"

Treacle had slipped his halter and galloped off. Joe snatched up the halter and caught up with Francie and together they chased after the donkey, skidding and sliding downhill. When at last Treacle paused, it was in the middle of a patch of stinging pinksap. He waited until Joe had the halter over his ears then he ducked away.

Finally, as the sky grew dark, Treacle allowed himself to be cornered and led back up the hill.

Joe was shaking with tiredness when he flopped down by the fire, legs and arms all scratched and itchy, for a dinner of burnt, sugar-less porridge.

"So, what happened?"

Sal told Joe what Beckett had said.

"I took a bit of cheese and some raisins," Joe admitted.

"So did I." Sal had calmed down and just looked sad.

"And me. A little bit. Actually, quite a lot of little bits of sugar," said Humph.

"So did Francie. We all did," said Joe, putting his arm around Humph.

"But we promised," said Sal. "And we haven't got much food. Beckett's right, we've got to ration it."

"And now we haven't got Beckett, because he can't trust us." There was an rock in Joe's throat. "We didn't think. We should've thought. We have to be able to trust each other."

"That's what I meant before," said Sal. "About having to think like a grown-up. I don't know if I can. Fourteen isn't old enough."

Joe shivered. The dark seemed darker and scarier than before. "I wish he was here."

"Tell him!" said Humphrey. "Shout."

Joe climbed onto a rock and shouted "Beckett! Beckett! We're sorry. Come back. Please!" as loudly as he could. His voice echoed down the dark valley into silence. Joe could usually see the bright side of everything, but going on without Beckett felt like a stomach-knotting, terrifying disaster.

"And we've still got twenty-one days to go," said Joe.

They put more wood on the fire and huddled together, but it was a long time before anyone slept.

"Joe? Joe?" Sal was shaking his shoulder.

"What? I'm asleep."

"We'll have to go back. We can't do it without him."

Joe rolled onto his side. He was surprised at how relieved he felt. "I know. In the morning. Back to Grand Prospect and find Ma. It was a stupid idea, anyway."

CHAPTER TEN

LAZY LUMMOCKS

But when they woke up, there was Beckett, squatting by the fire making porridge.

"A second chance," he said as he stirred the pot. "Because I really want that railway and Francie's maps are the only way to make that happen. But it's like this. If we can get to New Coalhaven in twenty-one days, there's enough for porridge every morning and one loaf of bread each day, so that's two slices of bread each for lunch. I can make the rest stretch to maybe fifteen dinners. And that's it." He looked them all in the eye.

"So some days we won't have dinner?" said Sal.

ROGER'S REGRET

Carrot swooped down onto Beckett's head, screeching, "Dinner!"

"Ouch!" Beckett detached the parrot and set her down on a bit of firewood. "Not unless we can catch a rabbit or a fish. *And* as long as we get to New Coalhaven in twenty-one days. If it takes any longer, there'll be no breakfast or lunch either. I think we can just make it. But only if you promise that you won't touch the supplies, and you mean it."

They promised, and this time they did mean it.

"Maybe we can kill a deer?" Joe said.

Beckett laughed. "Let me know when you've cornered one and I'll crack it over the head with the spade."

"We realised we couldn't do it without you," said Sal, "so we'd decided to go back—but now … Joe?"

The sun was shining and Joe's legs felt strong again.

"Onwards!"

Francie clapped.

"Then let's have breakfast!" said Beckett.

While they ate, Joe told them about seeing Roger and his Ruffians resting between his markers. "It shows they must think this is a good way to come."

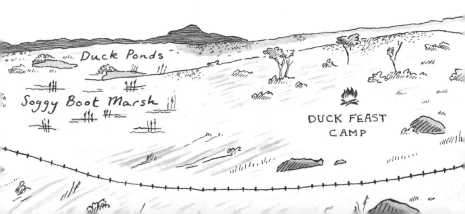

"Maybe we can follow their markers for a bit," suggested Beckett.

They loaded up the donkeys and slogged up to the ridge. There was no wind and once again Joe was dripping with sweat as he climbed. Humphrey led the way, always the first one to spot the orange strips that hung from branches to beckon them on. The others followed in a long straggly line, with Sal and the altimeter at the back.

They rested at the top and admired the way they'd come and tried not to think about how far there was to go. Joe's markers led into the broad valley, which stretched north for miles with Crocodile Ridge to the right.

Beckett squinted into the distance then looked at Joe. "What did you call this valley?"

"Treeless Valley. Because it is."

"Treeless." Beckett kept looking at Joe. "So, how do you think we'll be cooking tonight?"

Beckett and Joe retraced their steps with Treacle, down and down, until they were in the forest again. "Why didn't you mention no trees?"

"Sorry, I didn't realise it was important." Joe piled up dead branches.

"Well, no, not if you don't mind going without meals, and eating your oats mixed with cold water. You need to think."

Joe was stung. "But I think all the time—about the way to go, and all the clues that come from plants and clouds and streams."

Beckett sighed. "Look, if we make it to New Coalhaven, it'll be because you and I keep thinking. I should have had my catapult ready. You should have remembered to say about needing to collect firewood. All right?"

Joe hadn't realised it before but it was true: Francie and Sal liked to be warm and dry but they wouldn't necessarily plan ahead to make that happen. They thought about maps and mathematics, which weren't really everyday things. Beckett was very good at everyday thinking, thank goodness, and he was right: Joe needed to be good at that, too.

"All right."

They piled fallen branches across Treacle's baskets.

"Just as well Humphrey likes walking," said Beckett. "No riding for him today."

One good thing happened while they were away getting wood: Francie made friends with Dumpling. Up until then she'd avoided the donkeys, but when Dumpling was standing quietly, Francie had moved closer. She'd understood something, and when Beckett got back she showed him the tube of salt. When he said yes, she shook some salt onto her hand for Dumpling to lick, and gave some to Treacle as well. She poured water into the bucket from the barrel and let them both drink, and when it was time to move again, she picked up Dumpling's halter, and Dumpling allowed herself to be led. Francie seemed to know when the donkeys needed to rest, and when they needed to be encouraged to keep moving. She watched where Dumpling preferred to put her hooves, leading her left or right to avoid soft ground or a too-big step up, and the donkeys seemed eager to follow her.

Now he didn't have to take charge of the donkeys, Beckett could roam. He disappeared that afternoon, and when he caught up again at dusk he was singing, "Three ducks swimming on a pond. But now there's only one."

He dropped two floppy ducks at Sal's feet. "I caught them. You can pluck them."

Joe thought Sal was going to throw them at Beckett, but she didn't, probably because she didn't like touching dead things. She glared at him, steadied one of the limp bodies under the toe of her boot, pinched her mouth and tugged at a tail feather. Nothing happened.

"Show us?" Joe asked quickly. "We'll do it, just show us."

Beckett sighed. "Reckon it's going to be a long time before we eat."

First they had to light a fire and boil some water, then they dunked the ducks in the water by their feet, so the feathers pulled out more easily. It took ages and there were still lots of tiny poky feathers sticking out of the skin. Beckett showed Joe how to burn them off with a stick from the fire, and he cut off the heads and the feet.

Then Beckett asked Sal if she was going to gut them.

She looked up from her notebook. "I'd rather starve."

"Suit yourself." Beckett pulled the birds' guts out.

"Stinky Malinky!" Carrot flapped away from the revolting smell. Joe grabbed the spade and buried the guts as fast as he could.

Beckett pricked the ducks' skin with the tip of his knife, then he wetted a straight stick and threaded it right through the ducks where their heads and tails had been. "Guess what? I saw those Ruffians of Roger Rumplebum. They're camped just back there.

They must've hidden and let us pass them. Now, why would they do that?"

Joe frowned. Why would they?

Sal jumped up. "I bet you a box of barley sugar that they're following your silks!"

"Stealing my route!" said Joe.

Beckett nodded and pushed a forked stick into the ground either side of the fire. "That's what I was figuring, too. Lazy lummocks. They'll follow your silks until the last minute and then they'll charge past us to the finish line." He looked thoughtful. "No hurry, but we may be needing a plan."

Humph pointed to a pinprick of red light to the south-west. The Ruffians' fire.

"Forget about them," said Beckett "Let's get these ducks roasting."

He balanced the ducks' stick on the two forks. The fat sizzled and spat onto the glowing coals and the smell of the roasting meat was, they all agreed, the most delicious smell in the whole world—even better than the smell of Beckett's bread baking.

When Beckett finally declared that the ducks were cooked, and shared the meat out into five bowls, Sal looked very relieved, and thanked him.

"Delicious. Bet those Rascals' dinner isn't half as good." Joe sucked the last bit of juicy deliciousness off every little bone. "You should open a restaurant, Beckett."

Beckett nodded. "I'd like that. Maybe I'll cook for the dining car on the train and when it steams through here, I'll remember these ducks."

Joe couldn't imagine a train crossing this wild moor. The donkeys whinnied in the darkness. The wind was getting up and the slice of moon kept disappearing behind clouds. Then far away something howled, and howled again.

"What was that?" whispered Humphrey.

"Maybe those Ruffians have a dog with them," said Beckett. "Whatever it is, it's a long way away."

Which was just as well, Joe thought, because it sounded like something fiercer than a dog.

Humph said he was going to tell a story. Humph's story went like this:

"Once upon a time there was a magic tent and every time you put it up you found something surprising in it."

"What sort of something?" asked Beckett.

"A chocolate pudding one time, and another time a chicken pie, and once a baby tiger."

"What happened to the baby tiger?" asked Joe.

"It said, 'Can I have some milk?' And it had some milk then it ran away to find its mother."

"Did it find its mother?" said Sal.

"Yes. Its mother was waiting for it at the top of a big tree and she hugged her baby tiger and said stop hiding in tents. The end."

"Craziest story I ever heard," said Beckett. "Twenty days to go."

CHAPTER ELEVEN

A BUCKET OF DONKEY DUNG

"I name you the Impenetrable Cliffs of Doom," said Beckett. It was a good name. As they got closer they could see that they really were impenetrable. There was no way through, round or over the wall of jagged cliffs.

Joe sighed. "Back we go."

Reluctantly they retraced their steps. They were nearly all the way back to where they'd eaten the ducks when Roger

Rumpledown materialised out of the heather and called to them. The rest of his team were lounging about by one of Joe's silks, playing a card game.

"Well, here you are at last. We saw you'd turned around by the cliffs so we waited. Not your best route, young Santander. You've wasted us half a day."

Joe tore his silk from the bush. "Did we ask you to follow us?"

Roger snorted with laughter, displaying a gold tooth. "Chop-chop now. No more dawdling."

The rest of the Ruffians glanced up from their game. "Yeah, hurry up, you lot," they called.

Sal was furious. "You are the rudest, laziest, most outrageous excuses for humans that ever existed." The men just laughed.

"Get on with your work," Carrot ordered. She flew down onto the playing cards, scattering them with her wings and claws. "Chop-chop." She danced around on the cards then flew up, out of reach of the men's grabbing hands, carrying the king of spades

in her beak and leaving a trail of white smears all over the cards on the ground.

Humphrey squealed with delight. "She plopped on them!"

The men jumped up, swearing and waving their fists, and one of them pulled out a pistol and fired it. There was pandemonium. Humph screamed and ran at the man with the gun, Beckett grabbed Humph and held him, kicking and wriggling; the donkeys bucked and brayed, men's voices boomed, and the white horse galloped in circles with Carrot riding on its nose.

The stolen card fluttered to the ground and as a Ruffian tried to snatch it up, the horse stood on his hand. Sal heard some swear words she'd never heard before.

She bellowed at the others to follow Francie, who was leading the donkeys away, and she planted herself in front of the man with the pistol.

"If you fire that thing again, you'll have to put a bullet through me. Come on, Carrot, we've got a race to win." Carrot flew to her hand.

"And you," Sal stabbed a finger towards Roger Rumpledown, "are a disgrace to explorers. You should be ashamed."

She was so angry she wouldn't have been surprised if a flame had blasted from her finger and scorched Roger Rumpledown, but no such luck. He just laughed at her as she hurried after the others.

"I could kill that man," said Joe.

"I just want to make him sorry," said Sal as soon as they were well out of earshot.

"We could stop marking the trail," said Beckett.

"But if we need to backtrack because of a dead end—like today—then we'll need the markers," said Joe. "And if our route gets chosen it'll help the surveyors."

"And for Ma coming," said Humph.

"Right." Beckett glanced back at the Ruffians. "Then what we need to do is to lead them astray."

By the time they'd found an easy path up onto Crocodile Ridge, they'd made a plan. They walked along the ridge for the rest of the day, and every time they had a clear view back they could see the Ruffians, trailing along in the distance behind them.

"Tomorrow they'll be sorry," said Joe. "Nineteen days to go."

The next morning, as soon as it was light enough to see, Joe set off down the side of the ridge with his rucksack, his silks and the bucket, which he'd filled with donkey dung. The others packed up the campsite and hid the donkeys in a cleft in the rock.

They watched from their hiding place as the Ruffians followed Joe's silks down the slope and disappeared under the trees. When they were safely out of sight the Santander team, minus Joe, set off again, being careful to stay below the ridgeline so they'd be harder to spot.

Meanwhile, Joe marked the false trail with his silks, and now and then shook a little pile of donkey dung out of the bucket. He led the Ruffians across a field of boulders that ended abruptly at a sheer drop, then down a gully that led to a river. Finally he tied a few silks along the river bank to tempt the Ruffians south, the opposite direction to the way they needed to go.

Joe was tired, and a very long way from the others. First, he needed to get back to the ridge. He started to climb. Up a steep bank, clinging on to roots and trunks. Out of the trees, breathless, arms aching. Up again, over rocks. Sore, sore, sore.

At last he was back at the top. Another half hour brought him to where the donkeys had been hidden, then he was following the real donkey dung trail, checking his compass often to be sure. Sometimes he caught a glimpse of the lake that Francie had drawn at the top of her sketch map after flying, shimmering in the distance to the north. She'd called it Finger Lake. That's where they were trying to get to tonight.

It was twilight when Carrot spotted him and flew, shrieking, from Beckett's shoulder to Joe's. Humphrey ran to hug him.

"Good work!" Beckett took the bucket. "One team far behind us. Just four to go."

Joe swayed with exhaustion, but they couldn't stop yet because the ground was squidgy under their boots—far too soggy to lay out the bedrolls. They had to keep going.

"You've got mettle, Joseph Santander. I'm impressed." Beckett gave Joe a handful of raisins and shooed Carrot away. "Go and find yourself some insects."

Joe grunted; he was too tired to speak. Almost too tired to chew. He just squelched on, legs aching, back aching, feet aching; left right, left right. Francie took one of his elbows and steered him gently.

Humph patted his hand. "Not much further. Good boy."

The stars and a fat slice of moon were out when they reached a raised patch of dry ground near a stream, almost at the lake.

Water and a camping place—but no wood for a fire. They could see a smudge of deeper darkness in the distance that was probably trees, but Joe couldn't manage another step.

"You can go on without me. I'm going to sleep here for at least a month."

"You'll feel better in the morning," said Sal. "Eighteen days to go."

When he woke in bright sunshine, Joe could hardly move. His muscles ached, his head throbbed and his face was tight with sunburn. He forced his feet into his boots again. Then he stood up on his protesting legs and made his feet follow the others over the springy grass towards the distant trees which grew beside Finger Lake. By the time he caught up they'd got a friendly fire burning and the porridge was on. While the billy boiled, Joe stripped off his clothes and jumped into the lake before he had time to change his mind. The water was freezing, but his head and his sunburn both felt instantly better, and when he'd eaten breakfast and drunk two cups of tea, the rest of him felt much better too.

Carrot flew down and perched on the toe of Beckett's boot and tugged at the lace. The soles of both boots were flapping loose and there was blood seeping out of the toe of one of his socks.

"Yikes," said Joe, who hadn't even noticed that Beckett was limping. He felt bad.

"It'll be all right. It's only a bit sore."

Sal peered at his boots. "But if your feet get infected you won't be able to walk and then we'll have to stop and we'll lose the race."

Beckett shook his head. "Don't know that I can cope with so much sympathy, Sal."

She scowled at him, but he did take his boots off. His feet were a dirty, bloody mess. He washed them as clean as he could, smeared salve over them, and bound them carefully with some of Joe's silks. Then he put his spare socks on, which didn't have any holes in yet, and Joe helped him bind a silk around each boot and tie it very tightly to hold the sole on.

Just as they finished Francie ran towards them beckoning frantically. Joe followed her under the trees that hung out over the water. She crouched in the shadows and put a finger against her lips. Joe squatted beside her and searched the lake. All quiet and still. The other side of the lake was quite close.

Then—a voice. A man's voice. Someone said what sounded like: "Not if my life depended on it".

Joe scanned the far bank. Some ducks flew up protesting as something passed beyond the reeds, something brown, something white above and behind. A person. Several people.

They ran back to the others.

"It's the Solemn men!" Joe called. "On the other side, moving fast. They've come this way. Francie saw them."

"You sure?" Sal screwed up her eyes against the bright morning sunlight. "We can't let them get ahead."

They raced to pack up the donkeys again, talking as quietly as they could. Joe grabbed the bucket. "That has to be good. It must mean that this is the best way. I'll put out the fire."

"Use the shovel and smother it," said Beckett. "Water makes too much smoke. Don't want them seeing us."

"It's good news for you." Sal passed Beckett the cooking pot to put into Dumpling's basket. "If this is the best direction they'll surely send the railway through your village and up the Brightwater. But it's bad for us."

Joe buried the fire under shovelfuls of dirt. "Why's it bad? It just proves we're the best at finding the best way."

"Think about it. The Solemns started out up the Prospect Valley." Sal stuffed a groundsheet in with the cooking pot. Beckett took it out again and folded it. "So they must have got here by travelling west over mountain passes when we were just going straight up the Brightwater Valley. They're moving much faster than us. They'll get to the finish line way before we do."

They hurried all that day. Humph rode on Treacle when he got tired, and they only stopped long enough for Francie to draw and for Sal to take essential measurements. In the afternoon the boys kept going when the girls stopped, and by the time the girls caught up at dusk, the boys had made a fire, taken care of the donkeys, spread the groundsheet, put dinner on to cook, and collected a bucket full of pugnuts, which Joe was cracking painstakingly between two stones. They'd only had a few raisins and a small piece of cheese since breakfast because of not making any bread the night before, so their stomachs were growling, but they remembered to ask Beckett and not sneak the nuts.

"Two each. Dinner's nearly ready."

Joe and Francie left Sal and Humph cracking nuts and took the bucket and water barrel down to the lake. Roosting birds were chattering in the trees, but the water was silent and still. At the head of the lake a mountain rose sheer to a snowy peak, all pink in the evening light. Below, spreading towards them across the water, was its mirror image, a perfect reflection.

"It's my turn and I'm going to call it Mt Leopold." Joe aimed a flat stone and sent Mt Leopold into ripples. "… ten, eleven, twelve jumps! That's my best ever."

Francie was rocking on her toes and squinting down the lake. There was something in the distance that he hadn't noticed before. A little island? It was getting bigger. It was moving. A bird? No, a boat!

It was a small boat, and it was moving fast, even though it had no sail and no oars. It was low to the water and it seemed to have a chimney that was puffing little clouds of smoke. The sound it made—a high-pitched wheeze above a growly *chug-chug*—became louder and louder, until it echoed off the cliffs of Mt Leopold. The others came running to see what the racket was and they all squatted under the willows and peered out across the darkening water.

There were two men in the boat.

Francie mimed smoking a pipe. Sir Monty's Mountaineers. One of them was steering at the back, and the other was standing at the front.

"The route-finder," said Joe.

As the boat passed them they could see it was powered by a wheel turning at the back.

"But what's turning the wheel?" whispered Sal.

"Steam," said Beckett. "There's a boiler in the middle, see? They feed wood into it, and the steam drives the crankshaft that turns the wheel. It's a paddle boat. Ingenious."

104

"So genius!" murmured Humphrey.

The boat puttered on towards the cliffs of Mt Leopold, then turned in a wide arc and returned down the lake.

"But how did they get the horses to carry all that?" said Sal.

"The boat folds. The boiler goes separately—it probably boils the water for their tea too. And I bet the paddle wheel packs flat and slots together." Beckett looked very pleased to have seen such superior technology.

"Clever, clever, clever," said Humphrey.

"They've still got to ride the mechanical horses all the way up the lake. We're way ahead of them," said Joe.

"I bet those mechanical horses gallop like the wind," Sal said gloomily. "Do you realise that even if we manage to finish this whole race we still might not win anything? I bet they have a map-drawing machine and their maps will be perfect."

Francie looked dismayed but Joe couldn't be bothered arguing because dinner was ready. When they'd eaten their rice and beans Beckett cleaned out the pot, put the shelled pugnuts in it and put it on the fire. He stirred them until they turned dark brown and smelled delicious then he pounded them to a paste and added some salt. He gave them each a lick.

"Pugnut butter. Tomorrow's sandwiches will be the best ever."

The night was black beyond the firelight, and a cold wind blew off the lake cutting through their clothes. They built up the fire and arranged their sleeping bags close together on one groundsheet, with the other groundsheet over the top of them, and wore their woolly hats, jerseys and socks to bed.

"Only seventeen days to go," said Joe.

CHAPTER TWELVE

QUITE A BIT SCARY

Sal was filling the barrel in the lake next morning when she heard *click-clack, click-clack*. She looked up just in time to see the Belgian tracking hound run, nose down, tail up, across the clearing on the opposite bank, followed by the mechanical horses. Something flashed from the first horse. There were two long blades angled out in front of it, slicing through saplings and small branches to clear a path for the rest. The blades must have been very sharp because the horse moved forward at a regular

Francesca Falls 2109 ft

Mt. Leopold

SECRET CAVE CAMP

trot. All the other red hooves rose and fell in a long line behind it; their joints click-clacked, and blue tails swung behind them. The inexhaustible horses were following the Solemn men's route along the other side of the lake, and they were going fast.

Humph and Francie were standing in the shallows cleaning out the porridge pot, and they watched the horses, too.

"There's only eleven people now, not twelve," Humph announced.

"So beautiful, and so fast!" Sal sat on the bank near Francie. "I didn't mean what I said last night, Francie. I know we haven't got a hope of getting to New Coalhaven first, really. And I know your maps will be the best. I just don't think we can get there in time."

Francie nodded but her face said *I think we can.*

Not long after the beautiful horses had vanished into the distance, one of Monty's Mountaineers stumbled along on foot, shouting, "Wait for me, damn it. Wait for me."

"There's number twelve. Why don't they wait for him?" Humph was deeply shocked.

Francie hugged him and Sal said, "Because they only care about being first. *An expedition should never go faster than the speed of its slowest member.* That's what Pa always says. Now let's all go fast."

They hurried all day. Beckett was limping and they were all tired and quiet when, late in the afternoon, they heard a roaring noise that gradually got louder and louder.

"Sounds like a huge river," said Sal apprehensively.

They came out of the trees into an open space and saw a ribbon of water sparkling up a cliff so high they had to crane their necks back to see the top.

Beckett whistled. "That must be the highest waterfall in the whole country!"

"Maybe the whole world," said Joe.

Sal unstrapped the legs of the theodolite. "I'll measure it."

A cloud of spray hung in front of the waterfall, but there was no lake or mighty river at its foot, just a small stream running through and under a field of sharp-edged, slime-covered rocks.

The sight and smell and energy of the waterfall—which Sal announced was 2109 feet high—washed away all their tiredness.

"Imagine it!" Beckett flung his arms out. "Two thousand one hundred and nine feet! Everyone's going to want to see this. The train will *have* to come this way!"

Francie finished the day's map and carefully printed 'Francesca Falls (2109 ft)', then she and Joe went exploring. They clambered over the rocks, picking their way towards the cliff-face until they were right beside the thundering water. The roar of it filled their heads; Joe hadn't imagined that anything in the natural world could be louder than machines. The noise didn't bother Francie at all, perhaps because it was all singing with one voice. She pointed to a misty gap between the blanket of water and the cliff behind. Her eyes gleamed.

Joe grinned, and they scrambled on together until they were right behind the waterfall. They were inside the booming, chest-shaking noise, where breathing was a struggle because a freezing wind whipped all the air away and replaced it with spray.

Joe could feel Francie fizzing with excitement, and then a small cloud that had been covering the evening sun floated away,

and sunlight dazzled and shimmered. Behind the waterfall where there'd been no colour, every drop of spray became a prism; Francie and Joe were surrounded by a million glittering circles of light. She looked as though she was going to burst out of her skin with happiness.

They held hands and helped each other over the slippery rocks, through the wind and the noise, until they were out the other side, heavy with water that streamed off their faces and clothes and hair. They slithered back over the boulders towards the others, but Joe slipped and found himself sitting up to his chest in a pool of rushing mountain water, which didn't even feel cold.

Sal took one look at their faces. "Show me?"

So they showed her, and Humphrey came too.

Beckett yelled "You're crazy!" when they all climbed towards the waterfall, but when they waited for him, he hurried after them, muttering, "This looks like a quick way to get dead."

Later, they sat around in their sleeping bags grinning at each other, while their clothes hissed and spat beside the fire.

"I've never been this clean in all my life," said Beckett.

"I didn't even know you could go behind a waterfall!" said Joe. "And the biggest ever! I feel like I could run all the way to New Coalhaven, it's magic."

"I do, too. It's like energy juice. It's not magic though, it's science," said Sal. "I bet those Solemns understand how it works. I just hope they think it's beautiful and astonishing as well as scientific. Sixteen days to go."

*

They needed every ounce of energy the next day when they climbed up above the tree line and made their way along a bleak and stony mountainside. The wind blew at their damp clothes, and grey clouds covered the sun. In the evening, tired, aching and grumpy, they unrolled their sleeping bags among the stones.

Francie went flying before it got dark.

Up. Beckett coaxing a fire. Joe holding the bucket for Dumpling. Sal cleaning the altimeter wheel. Humph caterpillaring around in his sleeping bag. Up more. Back. The waterfall, and the long finger of the lake. Far, far down the lake some movement: a white horse. The Ruffians. Still coming, but days behind.

Around. Up high above the others. Such a jumble of jagged peaks, their tops all covered by cloud. And the valleys come together from every direction, no clear way on. Peaks, saddles, cliffs, rivers. Joe will decide. And down between the trees, a smudge of smoke. Another team.

This was officially a no-dinner night, but Beckett had made bacon and bean soup because the bacon was becoming smelly. It tasted very good. They cleared away the biggest rocks to make a space to lie down, but there were still a lot of small, jabbing pebbles and stones with sharp edges. Francie fell asleep straight away but the others couldn't get comfortable.

"Blooming stones," said Sal.

"I've got a good story about a stone," said Beckett. "But it's scary."

"I like scary," said Humph.

"All right, then. This one will make all your hairs stand up straight. And it's true …

"Once upon a time there was a young orphan called Tom who went in search of adventure. He needed to cross the Perilous Mountains, and knowing how dangerous they were he joined a group of travellers who were going in the same direction. The paths were steep and the weather was always stormy, and, also, an ogre called Stoneheart lived in those mountains."

"I especially like ogre stories," said Humph, sounding less confident. Beyond the firelight there was nothing but blackness.

"The travellers walked for many days, until they were cold and exhausted and starving hungry. Then one evening they saw a light in the distance, just as it began to get dark. A raging river ran along one side of the track, but as they grew closer they saw that the light was a lantern shining out of the window of an inn, and the inn was on their side of the river.

"A friendly innkeeper flung open the door in welcome and showed them to comfortable bedrooms.

"'You'll find lots of spare clothes in the cupboard,' he said. 'Help yourselves, get warm and dry, then come and have dinner. You look as if you need feeding up.'

"There were wonderful cooking smells coming from the

kitchen, so the travellers quickly washed and pulled on dry socks and dry clothes from the cupboard, and hurried to the dining table where the innkeeper served them the most delicious feast.

"First they ate a paté, but Tom thought it smelled strange so he only ate the bread that came with it. Then they ate roast goose, but Tom thought it looked strange so he only ate the potatoes. Then they ate pork, but Tom thought it smelled *and* looked strange so he only ate the baked apple. The others all drank a red wine that the innkeeper poured for them, except Tom, who drank only water.

"'What tender pork,' the other travellers cried. 'What fine goose, what flavoursome paté! What do you feed your animals that they taste so wonderful?'

"The innkeeper smiled a not altogether pleasant smile. 'Aha,' he said, 'That's a secret I cannot tell you.'

"They all went to sleep full and happy, except for Tom. The moon was too bright, he wasn't used to sleeping in a soft bed, and he was still hungry.

"Then, while he lay awake, he heard a strange noise: *whoop-whup, whoop-whup*. He tiptoed out of bed, down the stairs, out of the back door, and round to the kitchen window. *Whoop-whup, whoop-whup*. The innkeeper was sharpening his knives. The bright blades flashed in the light of the fire and the innkeeper's giant shadow moved across the kitchen ceiling. And then the innkeeper turned towards Tom. He had taken off his apron, and in the place where his chest should be there was nothing but an empty cavity.

"His heart was in his hand, and he was using it to sharpen his knives.

"Tom ducked down below the window. This was no inn-keeper, and this was no inn. They were in the house of the ogre Stoneheart! He tiptoed back inside to warn the others, more quietly than any mouse. But no matter how hard he shook them, his travelling companions wouldn't wake because they had been drugged by the ogre's wine.

"Tom heard the ogre's heavy footsteps on the stairs so, quick as a flash, he climbed out of the window and jumped down into the garden. He hid behind the rain barrel as the ogre came out into the yard carrying a lantern. The ogre hung up the light, then he lifted a trapdoor in the yard. He went back into the inn and returned with a sleeping body under each arm, and dropped them, one, two, through the trapdoor into the cellar. Backwards and forwards he went until all Tom's travelling companions except one had been dumped down the barrel-slide. The last one was beginning to wake up. He was mumbling and kicking. The ogre slammed the cellar door shut and carried the last traveller into the kitchen.

"Silently, Tom pulled open the cellar door, and threw a bucket of cold water onto the snoring bodies inside to wake them. Quickly, quickly, he untied the ogre's clothesline and knotted one end to the heavy iron boot scraper beside the back door.

"Taking a big breath he called out, 'Are you there, Stoneheart?'

"The ogre came roaring out, Tom pulled the clothesline tight, and the ogre tripped over it and tumbled to the ground. Fast as lightning, Tom wrapped the clothesline round and round the ogre's thrashing legs and tied him up. When the other travellers climbed out of the cellar, Tom told them to open all the garden gates, freeing the geese and the pigs from their pens. The animals ran out snorting and squawking and charged at the ogre. He howled in fright and pulled one leg free, stumbled to his feet, and hobbled down the road as fast as he could, pulling the boot scraper behind him. The animals chased him all the way to the raging river; Stoneheart saw them coming up behind him and he jumped. There was an almighty splash and Stoneheart was never seen or heard of again."

A stick cracked in the fire and Humphrey squeaked. "That's quite a bit scary, that story."

"What happened to Tom?" asked Joe.

"He carried on over the mountains to safety. Tom was my great-great-great grandfather. It's a true story—and I can prove it. See?"

Beckett took something from his pocket and stretched his hand out in the firelight. A heart-shaped stone. "It's been passed down my family. I sharpen my pocket knife on it."

Humphrey touched the stone with a cautious finger. "Is he truly dead? The ogre?"

"Dead as a doornail," said Beckett.

"You cook our dinner," said Humph uncertainly.

"But I'm not an ogre," said Beckett.

"What a good story!" Sal shivered. "Scary. Fifteen days to go."

CHAPTER THIRTEEN

THE HORSE'S TREASURE

Joe climbed up to the top of what Humphrey had insisted on naming Elephant's Ridge, and saw the confusion of valleys that Francie had sketched for him. Which way to go? They'd have to scramble all the way down a thickly forested slope to the valley floor, cross the river at the bottom, somehow, climb up the other side and go along, then up, then over the next ridge—which was

Mt. Elephant
5172 ft.

even higher and had snow on the top. Two short tunnels and a bridge could take the train through, but the path would have to zigzag endlessly up and down.

They still had a long way to go.

He met the others coming up the saddle. They were hot and sweaty and pleased because they were nearly at the top, but plodded on in disappointed silence when he led them straight down the other side.

"Keep a lookout for Stoneheart, Humph!" said Joe.

Humph looked around wildly. "But he's dead. Beckett said."

"Beckett *thinks* he's dead because he was never seen again. But maybe he just swam across the river and built another house."

"Joe's teasing," said Sal. "Take no notice."

Joe slammed the slasher through ropey crabstitch creeper. "Who needs mechanical horses, anyway?" He was tired and hungry and didn't feel like being kind to anyone. "Me."

He slashed through stickleweed, spear grass and spineythorn. "Die, die, die."

"Three sevens? Six nines?" screeched Carrot, who was clinging on to Joe's shoulder as he pulled aside the undergrowth.

"A million and one." Joe checked his compass. They were further west than he wanted, but that couldn't be helped. Down and down. It was even harder work than going up. His knees were sore and he'd run out of breath for talking or singing. They all became covered in mud as they slipped and slithered down his zigzag track, and their boots got heavier and heavier. Joe's heart sank as he heard the ominous sound of rushing water and caught a glimpse of a wild river through the trees.

At last the ground flattened out.

Joe called back to Beckett, "Are donkeys good swimmers?"

"They'll probably swim to save themselves, but I can't."

"Nor can Humph," said Sal.

They pushed out of the forest to the bank of a river that flowed fast between great boulders, white water exploding everywhere in a series of cascades. Even a good swimmer would get pummelled to death, or forced head down between the rocks, if they fell in.

Sal looked around in despair. "We'll to have to go back up. Find another way down."

Beckett said, "Back up? I'd rather drown," and stomped off.

Humph threw himself to the ground. "You said nearly there. You said!" he wailed. "I hate you all. I only want Ma."

Then Sal lost it, too. "Don't be a such a total baby," she shouted. "At least you get to ride some of the way. I want Ma, too, you know. I wish we hadn't started this stupid journey."

Joe flopped down on a mattress of thick comfy moss. It was waterlogged—he might as well have been lying in a puddle—but he was so wet and muddy already he didn't care. He closed his eyes; he wanted sleep and more sleep, followed by a great big plate of steaming dinner, or the other way around, and there was absolutely no way he was going back up that mountain.

The river thundered, Humph cried, Sal yelled, then said she was sorry, then yelled again when he didn't stop crying. Something snapped. More snaps. Some crackling. A hiss.

Joe opened one eye. Francie had lit a fire—her first ever. She'd done it the Francie way. She'd made a perfect circle of identically sized river stones, then she'd broken a dead branch into pieces all the same length and built the fire with them. She'd found two forked branches and stuck them into the ground either side of the fire, so their forks were the same height. She'd stripped the twigs off another branch, wetted it so it wouldn't burn, and sat it across the forked sticks with the billy hanging from it.

Joe struggled to his feet, told her it was the most elegant fire anyone had ever made, and stuck his sodden back near its warmth. Francie looked pleased with herself, and when the billy boiled she made tea and filled their mugs.

Beckett came back. "I thought I smelled smoke."

"Time for sugar biscuits?" Joe said, at the same moment as Sal. They laughed then they both said "Sorry for being grumpy", at the same time. Joe was used to twin moments with Francie but he'd never been twin-like with Sal before. It warmed his insides.

"Sugar biscuits! At last!" Humphrey ran to find the tin.

Ma's sugar biscuits were rock hard. They were big and had to be sucked, not bitten or chewed, and they were the best treat ever for someone who was exhausted.

"We'll be able to cross somewhere," said Joe. "We just have to fight our way down-river until we find the right place."

Francie had map-work to do and Sal wanted to look at the altimeter. Humph had curled up under a tree with his thumb in his mouth, so Joe and Beckett went downstream to look for a place where the water was calmer. They'd been pushing their way through the undergrowth along the riverbank for ages and Joe was about to say, maybe they should try upstream instead, when they came to a large area of churned-up mud. There was a patch of scarlet under the ferns ahead.

It was a mechanical horse.

"Busticated." Humph poked a finger inside the hollow at the back of the horse's leg, which lay apart from the rest of the metal animal. He pulled out some rigid wire, and the end of a spring, and tested the hinge at the knee. While he investigated the horse, the others searched through its abandoned load to see if they could salvage anything useful.

The first box contained books, mostly by Sir Monty himself. "*Vanquishing the Desolo Desert* and *Conquering the Peaks of the Meru Manaya*. For goodness' sake!" Sal threw them back in the box, then picked one out again. "Actually, no. We can use the pages for toilet paper."

Beckett shook a pile of clothes out of a duffel bag. "A tailcoat! And a boiled shirt! Imagine taking fancy nob-wear on a race!"

His own red-check shirt was more hole than cloth so he swapped it for the stiff-fronted white cotton, buttoned the nob braces to his trousers to replace the string he'd been using for a belt and slipped his arms into the tailcoat. Then he pulled out a shiny black disc and waved it in the air. The crown popped out and, hey presto, it was a collapsible top hat.

Beckett put it on, stuck his thumbs in his braces and bowed. "Good afternoon, ladies and gentlemen. How do you do?" His posh accent was very convincing.

"How, how, how?" Carrot shrieked from her perch on the mechanical horse's rump.

"Now you just need some new boots," said Joe.

Beckett folded the empty duffel bag. "Waterproof. We can keep the food in it."

Francie was busy yanking the pins out of a collection of butterflies she'd found arranged on a board. She held the delicate bodies on her palm and let the breeze take them.

"Look." Sal opened a wooden box labelled *Hudson's Patented Clippers*. It had gadgets in slots marked for Fingernails, Toenails, Moustache, Beard, Nasal Hair and Ear Hair.

The idea of bringing special clippers for nose hairs made them all laugh so much that Sal and Joe had to wipe away tears and Beckett got hiccups.

Sal recovered first. "We'd better keep going. We don't need any of this stuff, and we still need to get across the river."

"Wait." Joe was rummaging through a crate containing silver cutlery, a tablecloth and—

"Treasure!"

Four bowls made of tin, with tin lids clipped onto them. They were heavy. They looked familiar.

"You know what I think these are?" He grinned at Sal.

"Puddings? Plum puddings!"

"You're a pudding!" said Joe.

The river bank had been horribly churned up by all the mechanical hooves and was just a strip of mud. Beckett was the first to lose his footing and fall flat on his back. Humph thought that was hilarious, until Beckett grabbed one of his ankles and pulled him down. Splat. Humph looked outraged for a moment then he started shrieking with laughter and rolling over and over until only the whites of his eyes gleamed from his mud cocoon. Joe gave Beckett a hand up and ended up face down in the mud himself; Sal hooted at him, so Joe threw a handful of mud at her, which she dodged, but skidded and sat down hard.

When they finally managed to slither and stagger on, exhausted from laughing, they were all caked in mud, except Francie, who was as sure-footed as the donkeys.

"Good thing mechanical horses don't poo," said Joe, setting Humph off into hysterics again.

They came to a place where the river broadened out into a wide pool above another series of rapids. The mechanical horses' tracks continued on this side but Joe knew that was taking them further from the way they needed to go.

"Let's try."

The river was still hurtling downhill, but the surface was smooth, and the bottom looked gravelly. No rock-hopping required, but it might be deep.

"It'll wash the mud off at least." It was starting to dry and was annoyingly itchy.

They had to get three swimmers, two non-swimmers and two donkeys across, plus their supplies, some of which—like the food and the maps—had to be kept completely dry.

Sal plonked herself down on the bank. "Don't talk to me, I'm going to do some thinking."

She sat in silence for a few minutes, squinting up at the trees, staring at their baggage and looking from one side of the river to the other.

"All right, I've worked it out."

The three swimmers, Sal, Francie and Joe, did rock-paper-scissors to see who would cross first. Joe won. They tied one end of the rope round his middle and threw the other end over the branch of a tree. Beckett let it out gradually as Joe walked into the water, prodding the riverbed in front of him with a stick to make sure there was somewhere to put his feet. The water was freezing and streaked with dissolving mud as it tugged at Joe's legs, then his waist, then his chest.

The current was faster than he expected and tried to snatch his legs out from under him. If he was swept over the rocks he wouldn't have a chance. He was being driven nearer to the edge. Then his stick prodded down into nothingness, was swept out of his hand, and ...

Bubbles, blackness.

He was tumbled over and over, his back scraped against something sharp. His arms and legs flailed. He felt Francie panicking. He was desperate for breath—but which way was up? Which way to air? He felt himself being pulled up and back by the rope. His hand banged against a branch; he closed his fingers around it, and pulled himself towards it with his last ounce of strength. His face popped up above the roiling surface and he coughed and spat, lungs burning, eyes streaming.

The branch stuck out from a small tree that was trapped between the rocks above the rapids. He kept a tight hold and hauled himself along it until his feet found the bottom, then he staggered through the shallows and collapsed onto the bank, coughing up water and shaking with cold and fright. He was across.

The others bellowed with relief, and cheered when Joe sat up. "Still alive!"

That was the first step in Sal's plan. When Joe stopped shaking he tied the rope to a tree trunk and Beckett did the same, to make a tight line just above the water. There wasn't much rope to spare.

Beckett and Sal unloaded the donkeys. Francie led Dumpling by her halter and made clicking sounds with her tongue and teeth. Dumpling seemed to understand because she followed Francie into the water without hesitating. Francie hung onto the rope with one hand and didn't lose her footing even when the water rushed up to her chin. Dumpling walked beside her and swam hard when the water lifted her hooves off the bottom.

Then Sal brought Humph over on her back. She lost her balance in the middle and they both went under, but she clung onto the rope and Humph clung onto her, and she was able to haul them both to dry land.

Humph inspected himself. "I'm nearly clean!"

Sal and Humph set about collecting wood and building a fire, and Francie gave Sal the box of matches she'd brought over, dry as dry, tucked into the mat of her hair. Then Francie and Joe went back together—to a screech of "Wrong way!" from Carrot.

This time, Francie led Treacle over, with Dumpling whinnying encouragement from the other side. When they were safely across, Joe unknotted the rope, climbed the tree and retied the rope to a higher branch so it sloped down to the far side of the river. Beckett had retrieved some of the wire, straps and buckles from the broken mechanical horse, and they used these to hang the loads from their flying fox. First up was a sack with the altimeter.

"Ready?" Joe yelled, and gave the sack a shove. It slid down into Sal's arms on the other side.

"Not even a splash!"

"No splashing on Humphrey River," shouted Humph.

"Humphrey River? Really? Then I name this Dead Horse Crossing." Beckett passed the rucksacks up and Joe buckled them over the rope and sent them safely across. Carrot watched with interest while Dumpling's basket with the surveying tools crossed, followed by Treacle's basket with the food. When the waterproof duffel bag holding the map tube zoomed down, Carrot was perched on top, feathers fluttering.

Then it was Beckett's turn. He climbed onto a lower branch, hung a strap over the rope, held on tight with both hands and pushed off. He hurtled down, feet trailing through the water because he was so tall. He was going so fast that for one awful moment Joe thought he was going to smash straight into the tree on the other side, but Sal threw a sleeping bag over the end of the rope just in time to break his slide.

The only thing left for Joe to do was to untie the rope and cross back over the river himself, but that turned out to be the hardest part of the whole day. He wriggled and pushed but the knot was immovable. He was balanced on a branch, stretching around another branch, trying to undo a knot that he couldn't even see properly, with fingers so wrinkled and cold there was no feeling left in them. The sun had long since gone from the river, and had nearly gone from the mountaintops too. His wet clothes clung to him, cold and clammy. The others were sitting in their sleeping bags drinking hot tea while their clothes dried around the fire, but Joe couldn't stop his teeth chattering.

Beckett shouted to him to cut the rope loose, and after a while even Sal yelled at him to cut it. Joe's pocketknife was in his pocket where it always lived, but even though his body was shaking, he remembered what his father had said about *always carry the longest rope you can*. He was determined not to shorten the rope any further. When Sal offered to come over and help, he yelled at her. What magic powers did she think she had over a knot? He needed something to poke the rope with. He climbed down and ran back to the mechanical horse and felt around in the gloom for something thin and sharp. A horseshoe nail would have been perfect but this metal horse didn't have shoes. He stabbed his finger on one of the butterfly pins and he sliced his thumb on a bit of loose metal, but eventually he prised a metal rod like a knitting needle out of the horse's broken leg.

He worked the skewer in between the tight fibres of the knot. He wriggled and jiggled, digging the point further in, trying to ignore the smell of steaming pudding that wafted over the river. It was so enticing that he thought he might drown in his own saliva.

Finally, he created a gap wide enough to get his frozen fingertip into, then a whole finger, and at last he was able to tease the knot apart and tie the rope round his middle.

"Pull me over," he called, and this time the river water felt warm to his exhausted, shivering body.

"You did it!" Sal gave Joe a hand, dripping, up the bank, and helped him get his wet clothes off.

When Beckett unclipped the lid of the pudding tin they were all overwhelmed by the cinnamon-y, clove-y, nutmeg-y smell of Christmas. The pudding was rich, dark and delicious but Joe found it hard to swallow because of the lump in his throat. The reminder of Christmas was a reminder of Ma and Pa and their old life as a family. He wasn't cold any more, and his stomach had food in it, but he was tired, and he was homesick and unbearably sad. He burrowed down into his sleeping bag, blinking away the tears that kept welling up behind his eyelids. Francie stroked his hair just like Ma did sometimes.

"Smells like rain in the air." Beckett pulled the top tarpaulin tight over them all. "And it's fourteen days to go."

CHAPTER FOURTEEN

TUMBLING DOWN— JUST LIKE THE RAIN

The rain was just a drizzle when they woke, but up in the mountains it must have been pouring, because the river was rising fast. Their crossing place was already a wild whirlpool.

"We were so lucky!" said Beckett.

Joe didn't feel lucky, he mostly felt miserable as he pulled his wet boots on over his damp socks and tried to tie the laces with cold fingers. Everything was sodden so the poor donkeys'

loads were heavier than ever. Beckett and Francie coaxed one donkey each. Carrot hitched a ride on Joe's head, under Ma's chimney-pot hat, her claws tickling his scalp.

Joe tried to work out which way to go. The train would go into a tunnel, but which way should the path go? He couldn't see far enough to be sure; all he knew was up and up. The valley side had sprouted small streams and waterfalls, and the donkeys needed a lot of urging before they'd slosh and stumble through the freezing water. Humph squelched behind Joe in his yellow oversized rain cape and Joe gave him a hand getting over the bigger streams. Everyone slithered and slid; their boots became heavy with mud again, and Sal had to keep stopping to scrape the mud off the wheel of the altimeter. They plodded on.

"Ladies and gentlemen," said Beckett, who had found a strong stick to help him walk, but was still limping on both feet. "Let me remind you why we are suffering this torture." He paused for breath, then carried on up the hill. "It's so nobody will have to walk this way ever again! Trains will take us everywhere!"

"Hooray!" said Humphrey.

HUMPH'S CAVE
OF
SALVATION

Crabstitch Forest

"In the future it'll only take one day to get through these mountains," Beckett continued. "And once there are trains, there'll be other engines too. These mountains won't be wild any more." He looked very happy with that thought. "There'll be inns and markets, everything modern and comfortable. And no more hard work for anyone. All the hard work will be done by machines."

"Like what?" Humph asked.

"Machines for harvesting and mining. Machines to chop trees into firewood, and for fetching water, and cooking. Maybe even a machine to carry me from my gate to the train."

"Machines for making machines?" said Humph.

"Bound to be! And if we want to see the view from the top of a mountain, a machine will just whisk us up there."

"A machine to pluck and gut ducks would be something," said Sal.

Joe called to Francie, "I want a flying machine so I can see what you see," and she smiled. They climbed on, more cheerfully.

The clouds swirled thicker as they climbed. Up and up. Then they were higher than the bush line, scrambling over rocks. The wind sent Beckett's top hat flying. He snatched it out of the air just in time, collapsed it and stowed it in his rucksack. Joe used his compass because he could only see a few yards ahead. On they went.

At last Joe arrived at what he hoped was the top. He thought he'd have a quick pee before the others caught up, so he put his gloves in his pocket and was fumbling at his belt with frozen fingers when the ground disappeared and he was falling.

He skidded and slid, faster and faster. At first he was on his feet, then on his back with stones showering down all around him, and then he was rolling over and over, desperately trying to grip onto something—anything—to break his fall. He stopped, thumping hard and painfully up against a boulder.

The sound of falling rocks died away and for a moment there was silence in the mist. He felt waves of fear and panic roll towards him from Francie. He checked that he was all right— legs worked, arms worked—then sent reassuring thoughts back to her.

The sound of Sal yelling and Humph screaming was muffled by the fog.

"I'm all right." His voice was just a whisper. He took a few breaths and tried again. "I'm all right. I think."

He couldn't see anything but thick white cloud. He turned cautiously onto his hands and knees. His hands were bleeding. His head felt empty—no hat. No Carrot.

He tried climbing up, digging his toes into the crumbly scree, but every move dislodged stones that skittered down the slope and then fell, lost in the silent void. Then he slithered back, too. He thought it was all over as one foot flailed out into nothing, but the other wedged up against the boulder. The fingers of his right hand found a lip of rock, and the left hand a tiny crack.

"You'll have to pull me up," he shouted.

"But how can we?" Sal's voice was shaky. "You've got the rope."

The coil of rope was still over Joe's shoulder. Maybe he could fix it to the boulder that had stopped his fall, but then the only way to go would be down into the misty nothing. He imagined his skeleton dangling at the end of the rope forever.

"Concentrate," he told himself.

Carrot landed on his head and massaged her claws into his scalp.

Up above, Sal's voice was getting more and more panicky. "You've got to think!"

"I can't even move." His voice quavered.

Humph said, "Francie's drawing an idea."

There was a moment's silence then a hubbub of voices again.

"But where's Carrot?" Beckett's voice.

"Here. Trying to make a hole in my head."

"There may be a way." Beckett again.

"Yes. You can do it! Good one, Francie." Sal.

"What? What?" Joe was getting cramps. The pain in his wedged foot was agonising; he had to shift his weight, but as soon as he moved his other foot he sent a shower of stones bouncing away into the abyss. Heart thumping, he shifted back to the way he'd been balanced before, but the leg that was holding him up was shaking now.

"Hurry. I can't balance here much longer."

They told him Francie's plan. It had to work. But first he'd have to get his rucksack round onto his front so he could open it, and hope that nothing had fallen out.

Slowly, gingerly, he shrugged one strap off his shoulder, then let go of the crack with his left hand for a moment while he slipped his arm through. He gripped it again and braced himself as the weight of his bag slid down his arm to hang from his right

elbow. Heavy. A good sign. He let go of the crack again and quickly reached under his tummy to pull the pack in under him. The hand clinging to the lip of rock was starting to shake too.

He heard his father's voice in his head: *Steady now, nice and easy, don't rush, Joe.*

His fingers felt their way into the outside pocket and found the bag of silks. No good. They were already cut and all too short. He managed to get the main bag unbuckled and slid his hand in. A candle. His mug. His spoon, and ... the ball of twine! He wriggled it up, pulled the end loose and held it between his teeth. Then he felt for Carrot.

"Good bird." He lifted her from his head and sat her on the rucksack.

"How you doing?" asked Sal.

To tie the twine around Carrot's leg he needed two hands. But he couldn't let go of the lip of rock.

"Trying."

His fingers were so cold he couldn't feel anything more than a dull throb. He tried to twitch the twine into a loop, and nudge another loop through but it flopped out.

"Still trying."

His hands were shaking too much. He tried again. And again. He couldn't do it.

"Idiot!" Carrot pecked at his hand and the end of the twine fell out of his stiff fingers. The parrot snatched it up in her beak.

"She's got it!"

From above came the rattle of the lid being taken off the raisin jar—a sound that was guaranteed to bring Carrot flying. Joe quickly unspooled the ball of twine.

Carrot looked him in the eye as if to say, "Leave it to me!" then she stretched her wings and flew up, a flash of orange in the mist. Shouted messages let him know that she'd delivered the twine and now all Joe had to do was tie the other end to the rope.

He leaned into the cliff-face and rested against it for a moment, then found the end of the rope and tried to knot the twine to it. It was impossible. He couldn't make his fingers do what he wanted; his whole body was shaking and his leg was agony. He fumbled, dropped the twine; managed to find it again, dropped the end of the rope. It was just too hard.

It flashed into his mind that there was an infinite drop behind him. He could just let go and in a few seconds it would all be over, but once again he heard his father's voice in his head saying, *Steady now. I know you can do it.*

This time he tucked the rope under his armpit, so the end stuck up near his mouth. Then he used his teeth and lips as well as his fingers to loop the twine around the bristly end.

Finally, he called to the others to pull, and the rope snaked up into the clouds. They pulled it all up, because they needed to make a loop in it.

"Just hurry." He felt faint. The shaking was worse. *You can do it; you can do it.*

And now the question was, would the rope be long enough? If it wasn't he was done for. Soon the others shouted that the rope was on the way down and at last the loop appeared, all ready to push his arms through, just above him.

"Give me a bit more?"

But that was all the rope there was.

He stretched. It was just out of reach. He tried to move his foot up the rock. For a horrible moment he thought his boot was wedged so tightly that even if he could reach the rope his foot would be trapped. He wriggled it until he felt the boot move.

He had to leave his boulder and haul himself up the half yard or so to the rope above him. Slowly, slowly he wormed his way up the crumbling cliff until one finger was hooked over the rope.

One chance.

"Brace yourselves," he called. "Three, two, one, go!"

Joe propelled himself upwards and shoved his arm through the loop. He was hanging from his elbow, then his other arm was through the loop and his head and shoulders followed.

"Pull!"

There was a scrum of arms and legs when he landed on solid ground at the top. Humph hugged his head and Francie hugged his shoulders fiercely. Sal started to yell at him for forgetting to take elementary precautions, but then Beckett called him a stupid lemming, and she turned on Beckett instead, and told him to shut up and that he hadn't got a clue.

"Sorry. Very sorry. I needed a pee, so stupid," Joe explained when he had some breath. "The rope was just long enough! And I nearly cut it last night. Lucky!"

"Lucky you didn't get your pants down, or your bum would be sore like your hands," said Humph.

They were sore. His nails were ripped and his palms and fingers were gashed and packed with grit. His knees and elbows were grazed, too.

"We need to clean those cuts," said Beckett.

"You'd be dead if it wasn't for Carrot," said Sal, who was sitting with her head between her knees.

"Ride on my shoulder, Carrot. Much safer," said Beckett.

"Joe, look!" squealed Humph. He was lying on his stomach looking over the edge.

"Get back!" Sal grabbed his ankle.

The cloud had parted and now they could see the skid marks Joe had made down the slope and the boulder he'd fallen against. It was the only thing that could have broken his fall on the entire cliff face. Beyond was a drop of hundreds, maybe thousands, of feet.

Beckett stepped back from the edge and sat down, trembling,

but Francie and Joe started shrieking with crazy laughter. Humph scowled at them and pummelled Joe with his fists. "You're a bit too lucky to be funny, you stupid Joe, you."

But they kept laughing hysterically until Sal bellowed: "Joseph Santander, you nearly killed yourself and ruined all our lives and now it's time to STOP BEING AN IDIOT."

Joe pulled himself together. Nearly dying wasn't funny, but still being alive was the best feeling he'd ever had, even though his hands were throbbing. And the only reason he was alive was because he'd taken the time to unknot the rope last night. Pa would be proud.

Time to get going. The clouds were blowing away fast and he could see which way they needed to go now. This was the saddle, the narrow ridge between two valleys. He'd got to the top and gone straight over and down the other side. Instead, they needed to make their way along the ridge, and part of the way down a spur, then up again and over another ridge where a field of snow glistened white on its flank. He imagined how good it would feel to push his throbbing hands into its coldness.

"Onwards, to the snow."

"I'm naming this saddle Joseph's Mistake," said Sal.

"Snow soon, Francie!" Humph beamed as if he'd arranged a special present for her.

"We must be about halfway," said Sal.

Beckett scratched Dumpling's nose. "Hear that? Halfway."

When he started walking again, Joe groaned. His whole body hurt now that the shock of the fall was wearing off. But at least it still worked. And he was alive!

He whistled to himself as he picked his way along the rocky spine of the mountain, and every now and then he threw a stone over the edge. The drop was so endless that he never heard it land.

The cloud had all blown away now and the view was astonishing. He loved being so high and seeing so far—it must be close to what Francie felt like when she flew. The world was vast from above, and so empty. Endless forested valleys, and crumples of grey mountains into the far distance. He couldn't see a single thing whichever way he looked that showed people had ever been on the earth. It felt strangely comforting to be reminded how enormous the earth was and that he was just a speck in it. It was the same feeling he got when he looked at the stars. So many, and so far away. And they'd be there forever and wouldn't even know that people existed. He liked that.

He stopped to watch a pair of huge eagles floating below them. He could see the markings on their backs—imagine being higher than eagles!

"Yee hah!" Joe leant against the wind until it was holding him up. "Hey, Francie! I'm flying, too!"

They found a spring when they left the ridge and Beckett helped Joe wash the dirt out of his grazes. Sal unpacked the first-aid bag and found the salve and two rolls of bandage, which Beckett wrapped around Joe's hands so they looked like fat paws.

"Lucky it wasn't Francie. She'd never be able to draw like this," said Joe.

"Francie would never have been so stupid," Beckett muttered.

The only thing whistling in the afternoon was the wind, which came at them head on. They were walking along the side of the valley now, which was more sheltered than the top, but the wind grew more and more ferocious until each step was a struggle. The day seemed to go on forever. Grit stung their eyes and they shivered in their still-damp clothes as they fought to put one foot in front of the other. Joe thought it might be easier to walk inside the forest below them, but when he investigated he found it was full of crabstitch and stinging pinksap as well as crashing branches. It was safer to battle the wind in the open—and surely somewhere there must be shelter?

Carrot was blown backwards when she tried to fly. She dug her claws into Joe's shoulder and screeched. The clouds were piling up, dark as the slates on the roof of their old house, when Humph spotted an opening in the cliff-face above them.

"Firewood," yelled Beckett against the howl of the wind and they all ran after him to the edge of the forest, where branches were lashing and leaves and twigs were flying everywhere.

CHAPTER FIFTEEN

TO THE SNOW

The world had never sounded so noisy: rain torrented beyond the cave opening, thunder crashed off the mountains, and wind wailed up the valley. Sal rearranged the clothes that were drying on the rope that they'd stretched across the cave near the fire.

"What kind of tents d'you think the Solemns have?" She spoke loudly against the storm.

"Scientific ones," said Joe.

"Maybe they're inflatable." Beckett was kneading tomorrow's dough, slap-slap, on the lid of the cooking pot.

"Maybe individual waterproof tubes, like chrysalises." Joe tried to pincer a piece of pudding with the tips of his fingers, which was tricky with his hands encased in fat paw bandages. Everyone else had finished eating, apart from the donkeys, who nosed

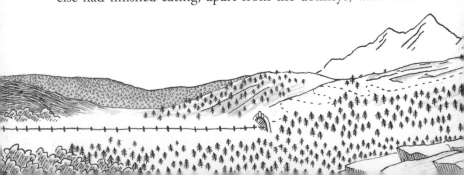

around unhappily at the back of the cave, looking for something edible among the branches that Sal and Beckett had piled up.

Beckett thumped the dough into the pot. "What I'm wondering is, how waterproof are mechanical horses? Has Sir Monty thought about rust?"

"And this wind would surely blow them over," said Sal.

"We're doing all right," said Beckett, stretching and tipping back his top hat, which made him look even taller.

"We are!" said Joe. "My route's great, and nobody's maps could be as good as Francie's."

Sal poked the fire. "Do you think that's true, Beckett?"

He shrugged. "I haven't seen many maps. But I reckon Francie's are good as any picture."

Sal nodded. "We had lots of maps in our house, made by our Ma, and our grandpa, and our great-grandma, and more great-greats, all the way back until when they invented paper practically. Francie's maps are way the most beautiful. I just hope my measurements are accurate."

Francie was drawing by the light of the lantern. She took no notice. Humph was drawing, too. He was drawing monsters

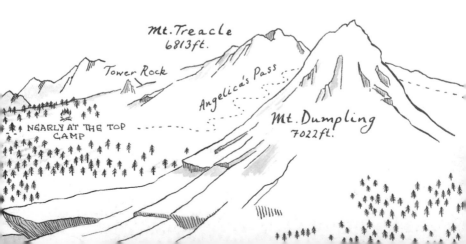

on the wall of the cave, with charcoal from the fire. "How many more days?"

"Thirteen," said Joe. "Thirteen days to go."

The next morning the storm was still raging. The rain stopped after breakfast, but the wind continued to howl and Beckett said it would be dangerous to go out.

"For goodness' sake, we can't afford to be scared of a bit of wind!" Sal said in her huffiest voice. Seconds later, an enormous tree went sailing past the cave opening. Her mouth hung open.

"Holygamoley!" She laughed. "Whoops, I take that back. Sorry, Beckett."

Joe tried to think whether he'd ever heard Sal admit to being wrong before. "The good thing is, everyone will have to stop for this storm," he said. "Not just us."

There was nothing for Joe to do, so he showed Humphrey how to write his name in charcoal, and Humph copied Joe's letters over and over.

Beckett mended his boots. He'd unpicked some strong thread from the mechanical horse's bridle and now he pulled it over a candle until it was well waxed, then he used the needle-for-getting-out-splinters from the first-aid bag, to painstakingly poke the thread through the empty stitch holes of his boots' seams. When he'd finished he rubbed candle grease into the seams of all their boots to help keep the water out.

Francie brought the maps up to date by the light of the lantern, and when the ink was dry she rolled them up carefully in their waterproof tube. Then she and Sal rubbed the donkeys down with rags torn from Beckett's old shirt. Sal hunted through the baskets for the hairbrush but it was definitely lost so she couldn't make them untangle their hair.

When the wind finally died down at sunset Joe and Francie volunteered to brave the pinksap and get more firewood. Francie led the donkeys and Joe ran ahead of her down the hill, glad to be outside and moving again.

There was fallen wood everywhere. Joe scooped up branches with his bandaged hands and Francie tied them into bundles and hung the bundles over the donkeys' backs.

They were on their way back up the hill when they heard a terrified scream from Humph, followed by Beckett's bellow. Joe froze, heart pounding in his throat, then raced towards the cave. Something flew out—larger than a rat, with great wings and claws. It was followed by another, and another. They had faces, and ears and hands. More and more poured out, and the air was filled with high-pitched squeaking. Thousands upon thousands of bats filled the sky in a dense funnel of dark wings that stretched from inside the cave to way above the forest.

Humph cannoned into Joe's legs. "Teeth! They've got teeth!"

Carrot shot out of the cave and flew round and round in frenzied circles, and Sal emerged with her hands over her head as the last bats joined the black cloud that was flying away over the forest.

"The cave roof just started to move! It came alive! How come we never saw them? They were hanging there all the time, millions of them!"

Beckett crossed his arms tight across his chest. "They suck blood. Vampires! I'm not going back in."

"They don't; they're good," said Joe. "I know about bats, our Pa told me, only I've never actually seen a flock of them before. They eat insects, not people, and they go out at night and come back at dawn. They probably only stayed at home last night because of the storm."

Beckett reluctantly returned to the cave, but only on the condition that they get up early in the morning and leave before the bats returned.

"Twelve days to go," said Joe.

He thought about bats as he waited for sleep. How could they fly so close together and never bump into each other? How could something be both a separate individual and also one-millionth of a swarm? What other creatures were like that? Ants? Bees? Those fish that swim in shoals? Were people?

*

The next day they climbed nearly all the way up to the saddle between two snow-covered peaks. It was Joe's turn to choose names and he called them Mt Treacle and Mt Dumpling, and the saddle "Angelica's Pass" after their mother.

They camped under a clump of pine trees below the snowline. Humph raced around squealing, "Snow tomorrow!"

Beckett unrolled Joe's bandages. "Dunno what magic's in your mother's salve but your hands look almost as good as my feet feel this evening."

Joe was happy he didn't need the bandages any more. For one thing, he could hold a spoon again, and for another he could put his gloves on and fit his hands in his pockets. The air was icy. They all wore their hats and jackets inside their sleeping bags.

In the middle of the night Francie shook Joe awake. They quietly laced on their boots and set off together in silence. The night was cloudless. The full moon hung low and its white light transformed the mountainside into something magical and mysterious. Their toes were freezing and their breath huffed out in small clouds as they climbed, but the moonlight reflecting off the snow ahead enticed them on.

They took off their gloves. At last they could touch it. It was crisp and icy, not fluffy at all.

"Maybe because it's old," said Joe. "Left from last winter. I think new snow's soft."

They trekked across the snowfield; Joe felt Francie's delight at the way her boots scrunched into it and at the trail of footprints that grew behind them. A small finger of a peak rose out of the snow and they started to climb. The moon was bright enough to see where to set their feet, up and up. It was a real climb, toes and fingers, but then they were sitting side by side on a rock on top of the world.

The view was so beautiful that Joe felt his eyes prickling. Everything was below them: there was the snowfield, and the glow of their fire; there the black reach of the forest and the silver glint of a river. Stretching into the distance were layers after layers of mountains all washed in moonlight, and a row of snow-clad peaks soaring out of the darkness on the eastern horizon.

The full moon hung so big and bright that he could barely make out any stars until he turned his back to the moon and looked towards the dark horizon where there were tens, then hundreds, then thousands of stars pulsing silently—chips of ice in an infinite, frozen world.

The night sky was the only thing Francie couldn't draw. She turned slowly, memorising the view, then opened her sketchbook and drew the silhouette of the mountains. She couldn't draw the night, but she could draw the light and the shadow.

"Eleven days to go," whispered Joe.

CHAPTER SIXTEEN

GOLDEN GLINTS

Humph was so excited about touching snow for the first time that he gobbled his porridge and urged everyone to hurry, but when they got close he spotted the footprints.

"Whose feet?" he roared.

Joe confessed that he and Francie had had an adventure in the night, and Humph was furious. He put his head down and ran at Joe, unbalancing him so he fell down backwards.

"Not, not, not fair. Francie and me were going to touch snow first together. You went without me. I hate you." He stomped

off across the snowfield and Beckett went after him. Sal accused Joe and Francie of being stupid and inconsiderate, so Joe didn't mention that they'd climbed the finger of rock; in the daylight it loomed sheer and unscaleable. He exchanged a grin with Francie that said, how on earth did we get up there? And safely down again?

Beckett piggybacked Humph back and dumped him at Sal's feet. "Guess what Humph's seen?"

"No, it's a secret," said Humph.

"Please? I'm sorry," said Joe.

"I saw the sea!" Humph announced.

"No! Really?" Joe put his hand up to shade his eyes.

"Yes, he's right, look!" shouted Sal. In the far distance, there was a glimpse of the sea, and a haze that must be the chimneys of New Coalhaven. Francie tugged at Joe's sleeve; she'd noticed something too. He squinted to where she was pointing. It was little more than a disturbance of the air. Smoke. Not so far away, another team was making breakfast.

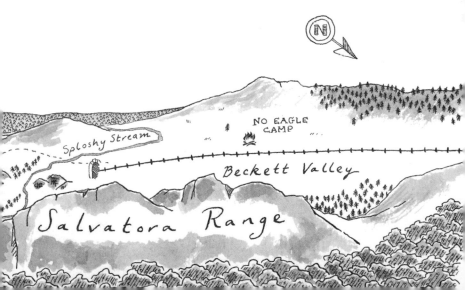

Which way? From their viewpoint at the top of the world Joe could see two valleys separated by the Salvatora Range. Both valleys looked as though they could lead towards New Coalhaven. Francie had to fly so they'd know which one led most directly to the sea. She'd need to sleep after flying and that would use up the rest of the morning, but Beckett told Joe:

"If we walked all the way down there and then you said, 'Sorry, we've got to go back up and go the other way,' I'd kill you. Slowly. And feed your liver to the eagles."

So they spent the morning looking down on the world. Sal took bearings from the peaks, Humph and Beckett made a snowman and Joe snoozed in a sheltered spot in the sun. Francie flew, then slept, after drawing a map that showed they should start off down the steep Beckett Valley that led west, towards a river that glowed golden in the sun.

That night, Joe found a campsite in a meadow of long grass with a tree in the middle to tether the donkeys to. As they waited for the billy to boil they listened to the donkeys ripping out mouthfuls of grass, and munching and snuffling happily to each other.

But people can't eat grass. Beckett had spent most of the afternoon trying to hit a bird with his catapult. There were some large birds gliding around above the mountainside, but they were too high; his stones all missed.

"Never mind. I bet they taste disgusting," said Joe. Still, after the thin soup they had for dinner, he was sorry there was no roast eagle to follow. He'd have eaten it, however disgusting.

Humph licked his bowl. "My tummy's still flapping. Can't we have a pudding?"

Beckett shook his head. "I'm saving the last one. But I think I saw some pugnut trees ahead, so we may get more dinner tomorrow."

"I know a story about someone who was hungry," said Sal.

"Is it scary?" asked Humph cautiously.

"No. It's got love in it, though."

Humph snorted but told her to go on anyway.

"This is a story our Ma often told us, but you may not remember. She heard it from her mother, who heard it from *her* mother. It goes like this:

"Once there was a young man called Griff, who fell in love with Mabli, a young woman who came to live in his village. Griff and Mabli wanted to get married but his father said, 'What will you live on? Neither of you has any money or the means to earn your living.'

"And Mabli's mother said, 'Griff has never left this village. He will always wonder what lies beyond it. You should send him away to see the world, Mabli. If he comes back after a year with money in his pocket, and you still feel the same about each other, then everyone will bless your marriage.'

"So Griff went off to see the world. He saw many wonders but he didn't meet anyone he liked half as well as Mabli.

"When the year was nearly up he had saved two gold pieces, which he hoped Mabli and her parents would think enough, and he started on his way home. He was so eager that he took a short cut through a great forest and before long he was lost. He walked and walked but soon he'd eaten all the food he was carrying, and he became very hungry. He looked under pugnut trees but animals had eaten all the nuts.

"Then he heard a cry and saw a hare caught in a trap by its leg. The young man knew that roast hare would taste delicious. He held the animal gently and was about to break its neck when he felt its heart beating fast under his hand. He realised he couldn't hurt it. So he spoke softly to the hare while he forced the teeth of the trap open, then he washed the bloody wound with water from his flask and let the hare go.

"The hare hopped a little way away then turned and faced Griff. There were strange golden glints in its eyes and it spoke to him. 'Young man, you have saved my life. I will grant you a wish.'

"Griff was astonished. 'I'm starving,' he said. 'I wish for some food.'

"The hare vanished, and in its place a picnic was laid out on a checked cloth. There was warm bread, a steaming bacon pie, a roast chicken, cheese pannikins, lemon dainties, plum pudding and all sorts of other delights.

"There was much more food than one man could eat so when Griff had eaten until he was bursting, he wrapped the leftovers in the cloth, slung the bundle over his shoulder and went on his way, full and happy. And the bundle was magic, for no matter how much he ate, there was always more food in the cloth when he unwrapped it.

"Some days later the young man came to an open heath where

there was no shelter from the howling wind. It snatched off his hat, and although Griff ran he couldn't catch it. Soon it began to snow. His ears became so cold that he thought perhaps he was freezing to death. Then he heard a squeal, from another hare caught in a trap. If he skinned it, its fur might keep his head from freezing so he could get home to Mabli. He put his hand on the animal and once again he felt its heart beating under his fingers and he knew he couldn't hurt it. So he forced the trap open and let the hare go.

"The hare hopped a short way off and stopped. It turned and looked at him with golden glints in its eyes. It said, 'Young man, you have saved my life. Now I will grant you a wish.'

"'My head is so cold,' said Griff. 'I wish I had a hat.'

"Then, *whoosh*—the hare disappeared and there was a warm woollen hat on the young man's head. And he was wearing new woollen trousers and shirt, and the lightest, warmest cloak was wrapped around his shoulders.

"Griff went on his way.

"Now there was only one more obstacle between Griff and his home: the great river that flowed through that country. Griff could see the smoke from the chimneys of his village on the other side, and felt his heart being tugged over the water as he hurried along the bank looking for a boatman to row him to the other shore. He walked until he came to a jetty, but there was no boatman there, and no boat to be seen. How would he ever get home to Mabli?

"Then he heard a shriek and saw a hare caught in a trap beside a hedge. He knelt down and was about to release the frightened

153

animal when an angry voice called out, 'Thief!' A man stood over him with a cudgel raised. 'That's my trap,' he snarled, 'and that's my hare.'

"'This trap is cruel,' said Griff. 'And you must let the hare live.'

"'I'll do no such thing,' said the man.

"Griff felt the hare's heart beating against his fingers. 'I'll pay you for it,' he said. And he felt in his pocket and brought out the two gold pieces. 'Here,' he said, 'this is all the money I have in the world.'

"The man called Griff an idiot and took the gold, and Griff knelt in front of the hare and forced open the trap. Once again he bathed the animal's wound, and let it go. The hare hopped away, then stopped and turned. It had golden glints in its eyes, and it said, 'Young man. You have saved my life, and in return I will grant you a wish.'

"Griff sighed. 'Oh, beautiful hare with golden eyes, what I want most in all the world is to get across the river to my beloved Mabli. But even if you could send a ferryboat this way, I can no longer pay for the crossing.'

"Then the hare vanished, and when Griff looked up, there was a new ferryboat sailing towards the jetty. And steering the boat was a young woman, the most wonderful woman in the whole world. It was Mabli.

"Mabli's parents were impressed that Griff had been so far and seen so much, and Griff's parents were impressed that Mabli had acquired a ferryboat that was desperately needed on that stretch of the river. So Mabli and Griff lived together happily for the rest of their lives, sailing that ferry across the river. And when the sun shone, Griff saw the golden glints in his wife's eyes, and he smiled and held her close, feeling her heart beating next to his. The end."

There was silence. Humph was asleep.

"That's a good story. I'll remember that one to tell my mother," said Beckett.

"You told that just like Ma," said Joe. He squeezed his eyes shut to stop himself thinking about how much he missed her.

"Only ten days to go, now," Sal whispered. "Goodnight, Ma."

CHAPTER SEVENTEEN

STRANDED

Joe had been hoping the forest would thin out, but instead they spent another whole day fighting the undergrowth to make a track, zigzagging endlessly down towards the river. Joe and Beckett took it in turns, one wielding the slasher and the other pulling away the creepers and prickle bushes that blocked their path.

"I'm sure we've done this already," Beckett grumbled. "This all looks the same. Couldn't we at least have blue leaves with pink spots, and purple and orange grass in some valleys?"

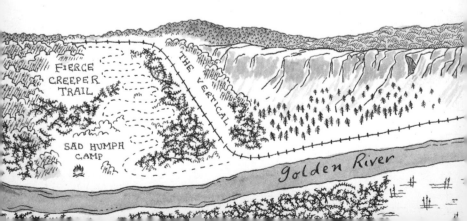

Francie clapped agreement. She and Humphrey were leading a donkey each with Sal at the back to make sure the altimeter kept turning as it bounced over tree roots and got tangled in ferns.

"Perfect for the Vertical. The climbing train will do this in a few minutes, but we've got to scramble blindly for hours," Sal muttered. "I hate not being able to see where I am or where I'm going. I hate not knowing what's round the next tree."

"More trees," said Beckett.

"Or a dragon," said Joe.

"Pugnuts!" said Humph, snatching one up from the ground.

"Hooray for Humphrey's noticing eyes!" said Beckett.

That night Sal announced that they'd descended over two thousand feet and walked sixteen miles.

"And we found a whole bucket of pugnuts," said Humph.

"Most of which still need cracking," said Beckett. He held out a pair of cracking stones. Francie took them. She immediately saw how to hit the nuts to make them split cleanly and she squatted by the fire and worked her way to the bottom of the bucket.

"You're a machine, Francie!" said Beckett. She smiled and did a jerky mechanical dance.

"Nine more days to go. Only nine more to go," Joe sang.

Later, in their sleeping bags, Humph rolled against Joe. "I'm feeling sad."

Joe hugged him. "We'll be there soon, and you'll see Ma."

"But why I'm sad is cos, when we get there, I won't be a venturing boy any more. I like being a venturing boy."

"I do, too," said Joe.

The next morning they reached what Francie had named Golden River when she was flying, but turned out to be disappointingly ordinary close up. They followed the river bank downstream. Humph was galloping ahead of the donkeys, whacking the tops off nettles with a stick, when Sal heard a voice.

"Wait, Humph. Stop."

Francie pointed through the trees. Sal hushed the boys and they moved forward together cautiously. The voices got louder, and angrier, and when they rounded a bend in the river they found themselves in a campsite. Rolled-up tents and bundles of belongings were strewn around and five of Monty's men stood by a smouldering fire looking furious. Four mechanical horses stood nearby with their heads hanging down between their front legs.

Carrot flew down to perch on one of them. "Chin up, shoulders back!"

The men stopped arguing with each other and turned on the Santanders instead.

"It's the ruddy kids!"

"*They* did it!" A bald man with a badly sunburned head started towards them. "What the blazes have you done with them?"

"I'll have your guts for garters, you ruddy saboteurs," barked another man, stabbing his pipe towards each of them in turn.

Francie let go of the donkeys and crouched down with her hands over her ears. Sal hated seeing Francie distressed, and her shoulders came up round her ears like a bull about to charge.

"Don't you dare shout at us!" she roared. "We haven't done anything. And we don't want to have anything to do with you. Come on!"

She grabbed Humphrey's hand and hurried past the men. The others tried to follow, but a third man stood in their way. He had a very red face, his sleeves were rolled up and his braces dangled, and he was panting as if he'd been running.

"Thief!" He grabbed Beckett by the neck of his shirt. "This is my dress shirt and my top hat! Ruddy thieving jackanapes."

"He isn't!" Humph broke free of Sal's hand and whacked the man's leg with his stick. "We found them. You throwed them away with your dead horse."

That made the rest of the men laugh, in a mean, sneering sort of way. "That's true, Gervais, your horse 'died'. You couldn't control it, could you?"

Gervais looked as if he were about to explode but he let Beckett go.

A man with an enormous moustache, who hadn't spoken yet, put a monocle in one eye as he approached Beckett. "Look here. Not a thief. Gervais abandoned his gear so, you know, fair's fair.

159

But we've got a more serious problem. A sabotage problem." He stood very close to Beckett and bent his head so they were almost nose-to-nose. His voice became an icy hiss.

"Thing is, someone's stolen our keys. What do you know about it?"

"Keys?" Beckett took a step back. "What kind of keys?"

The man narrowed his eyes. "Winding keys. Gone."

Sal was interested despite herself. "Is that how the horses are powered? I wouldn't have thought you could get enough torque, but I did wonder…"

"Oh, for God's sake, **WHAT HAVE YOU DONE WITH OUR KEYS?**" bellowed the bald, sunburned man.

Beckett shrugged. "If someone took them, it wasn't us."

The one called Gervais turned on the other men. "I told you, didn't I?" He laughed a bitter, snorting laugh. "I said. It's a Cowboy job. These kids aren't the competition—and they *were* way behind us. It's that blasted Cody Cole trying to stop us."

The anger seemed to go out of the men. They returned to the problem of how to get the horses going.

"Can't you use one of the other horses' keys?" Joe suggested. "They can't be that far ahead."

"We are waiting," hissed the icy man, "for such a key to be brought to us so we may continue."

"Unless each horse has an individual key. Not interchangeable," Sal pointed out.

"That would be a problem, all right," said Beckett happily. He gave Francie a hand up and led her past the men.

"You'd all have to walk. As I have to." Gervais sounded pleased.

"Well, good luck and all that." Sal sidled out of the men's reach.

"What nobs!" said Joe, when they were out of earshot.

Sal felt very cheered to know that at least part of Monty's team was behind them. But she was confused. "Those men are rich and posh. How come they're so stupid?"

"Money's got more to do with luck than brains," said Beckett. "And my mother says that nobs have often had the brains bred out of them. Like pocket dogs, or some racehorses."

They were even more cheerful when Beckett pointed to a cluster of very tall pines ahead.

"You know what they are?"

"Trees?" suggested Humphrey.

"Queen Pines," said Beckett. "And what do you find under Queen Pines?"

He scuffled in the pine needles.

"Mushrooms!" he crowed, waving a fungus as big as his hand. "And unlike pugnuts, they don't need cracking."

In just a few minutes they'd found enough mushrooms to fill the bucket.

"You're quite sure they're okay to eat?" asked Sal. "How can you tell?"

Beckett showed her how to check the gills under the cap. "We pick them every summer and dry them for the winter. Eat them until we bust."

That night they had a mushroom and pugnut stew, and it tasted meaty, thick and delicious.

"I wouldn't mind eating that every day for the rest of my life," said Joe.

"There's enough for tomorrow," said Beckett.

"Just imagine if you hadn't come with us," said Sal.

"I know," said Beckett. "Eight days to go."

The route ahead was straightforward: down the valley. But the ground became marshy and every path Joe made seemed to lead them knee-deep into bog. The railway would need firmer ground. When they found a dry hillock the others decided to stay put and bring the maps up to date. Joe could go ahead and find the route and they'd follow his silks in a couple of hours.

So Joe left the river and set off for higher ground, up over a spur and down the other side. But he soon found himself in a marsh again, with reeds and ponds and mud stretching into the distance to the left and right and straight ahead.

"Back again," he said to Carrot.

"Again, again," said Carrot.

Joe backtracked, untying his silks as he retraced his route: up the hill into a patch of gnarly old forest, back past the spruce that was leaning on a suswatch, past the beech tree with a hole right through its middle—and then the silks stopped.

Pa's voice in his head reminded him: *take it slowly, spiral out, keep the last silk in sight*, but he still couldn't see another one. And then the last one was out of sight too, and nothing was familiar. But there was a strange smell of burning leaves in the air. A camp fire? No. Pipe smoke.

Some of Monty's men must be nearby.

He tried all the tricks Pa had told him but he couldn't find his silks again. He was lost. Pa had warned him this might happen. He must use his compass and he'd eventually come across his trail of silks, then all he'd have to do is look for footprints and donkey tracks to know whether the others were ahead or behind.

Out of the corner of his eye he spotted something orange through the leaves. He hurried towards it—was it a leaf? No. A silk, and there was another. South-west, that was right. But the trees here weren't familiar. He must have forgotten. The ground sloped steeply; he was in a gorge. On? Or back? He had to hurry, he'd wasted so much time. Straight on was the right direction, according to his compass, and he hated having to backtrack, so he scrabbled down through the trees towards another flash of orange. Then the slope became really steep. Too steep for a track. He should really clamber all the way back up, but he was tired, and suppose this was a place where a bridge could go straight across? He ought to check it out, using the rope.

He looped the rope around a tree and gradually lowered himself down its length until he landed on a ledge. He could hear rushing water. He left the rope hanging and pushed the bushes aside, and there was the river. It filled the gorge; there was no crossing it, and nowhere to go. A bridge could easily take the railway over the top, but he'd have to climb back up to get out.

But the rope was no longer looped around anything; it lay sprawled across the ledge at his feet. It hadn't fallen by itself. Someone had thrown it down. The same someone who had moved his silks. A pipe-smoking saboteur.

Joe angrily coiled the rope and shoved it into his pack.

He hauled himself up onto the saplings that grew out of the bottom of the cliff, but then there was nothing. Nothing to hold onto, nowhere to put his feet, and the cliff-face just crumbled away under his hands.

He was almost crying with frustration. There had to be another way out.

Water was smashing and boiling through the narrow gap between the rocks. He could see a place downstream where huge boulders stuck up above the river; he might be able to step from one to the next. But there was a jungle of bramble bush growing down the cliff that he had to hack through first. He unbuckled the slasher from the back of his rucksack—slashing was exactly what he felt like doing.

"Scoundralous scanderoons." Slash.

"Rapacious rapparees." Smash.

Every branch of bramble he hauled out of the way was another of Monty's men lying bleeding and begging for mercy at his feet.

"Contemptible clotmongers." Crash.

It took ages to clear a way along the ledge, and when he got past, scratched and bleeding, he saw it was no good. The gap between the rocks was too big to leap. And even if he could have crossed the river, there was nowhere to land. A few bushes clung to the cliff-face, which looked just as steep as the side he was on.

Joe was furious with himself for not turning back when he could. But he was even more furious with Monty's men who had stranded him with a torrent below, a cliff above, scratch-arm behind and no way out. And it was getting dark. No one would find him now. He would have to spend the night on the ledge, alone.

He tied one end of the rope around the saplings, and the other around his middle, just in case he rolled in his sleep, then he wriggled into his sleeping bag and tried to make himself comfortable. On rocks. With an empty, growling stomach.

Joe thought about Francie. She'd know he was still alive and she'd make sure Sal knew too, but that wouldn't stop Sal being worried. She'd worry about him being lost and worry about not getting to the finishing line in time. Humph would be desperate: first his father disappears, then his mother, and now his brother. He thought about the stones digging into his back and the bliss of a fat mattress. He wondered whether the others would decide to stay put, or set off to search for him in the morning. He thought about the mushroom and pugnut stew that the others would be eating, and he even thought fondly about porridge.

He thought about Ma. Where was she now? Maybe she'd hired herself a strong horse and ridden day and night in hot pursuit. He hoped she hadn't because how would she cross that river on her own? And what if she met the bear? He hoped that she'd trusted them to get to New Coalhaven and travelled the long way around by boat. Maybe she'd be waiting for them.

And Pa. How many months had he been gone? Joe had lost track. But worse, much worse, was that his memory of him was fading. For the first time ever, he couldn't make Pa's face float in front of his closed eyelids. He could describe him in words: dark curly hair beginning to go a bit grey; bushy eyebrows, a full beard and moustache that hid his mouth, but you could still see his smile because it crinkled up his cheeks and creased his eyes. Which were brown. But the picture was blurred. He couldn't see Pa's smile any more.

Ma was all movement: pot on the fire, pass the spoon, washing basket down, kindling up, wipe Humph's face, stir the pot … but Pa was almost still. One thing at a time; no hurry. He'd collect up the boots, the cloth, the brush, the grease pot, the bucket of warm water, the soap. Then he'd sit on the step, take out the laces, wipe off the dirt, rub in the grease, brush it into the stitching, turn the boot, check the sole, put it down gently, take up its twin, until twelve clean boots stood in a line. Next, he'd wash the laces and pull each one through his fingers to squeeze out the water before threading them back criss-cross. Somehow the ends always came out the same length.

They wouldn't win anything now. Beckett's family would probably starve. Sal would have to go into service as a house-maid—which she'd do really badly so everyone would always be cross with her. Francie would get a job as an artist but she'd have no one to love her and look after her. And Pa would stay lost forever, and it would be all Joe's fault.

Or maybe the others would just go on without him, and he'd starve to death on this ledge. Serve him right.

He curled up in his sleeping bag and cried. Then his quiet sobbing turned into a howl and he heard the echo of his howl bounce back at him, over the noise of the river. He sat up and howled louder, then louder still, like a wolf. He howled until he had no more breath. Then he wiped his eyes and saw moonlight slanting into the gorge and washing over the far cliff. The river was dark below him but the water that splashed up gleamed, and the pale bark of the birch trees sliced the cliff-face opposite with shimmering cuts of silver.

He blew his nose on the tail of his shirt and had a drink of water, and was about to lie down again when he saw a shape on the rocks on the other side of the river. Sitting on its haunches, facing him, was a great silvery wolf. It didn't move but just twitched its ears and listened. It looked at him, and he looked back. Then it stood up and stretched and walked a few paces. As it turned, it looked at him again, then trotted up a path that slanted up the side of the cliff. Its silvery coat flashed between the darkness of bushes as it rose away to the left, until it was above the gorge. It paused at the top, silhouetted on the skyline, sang a long swooping note, then disappeared into the moonlit night.

The silver wolf had come to find him, had come to show him he wasn't trapped. There was a secret path up the cliff—if he could cross the river.

Seven days to go.

Joe tumbled into a deep sleep. He dreamed he was under water, unable to breathe, being swept along with his hair floating all around him like seaweed.

CHAPTER EIGHTEEN

FANTABULOUS FISH

Joe woke shivering, just as the dark night became the grey dawn. He knew exactly what he had to do. He chopped down all the saplings he could reach, and one at a time he stripped their branches with his slasher and lowered the trunks across the river. Just one sapling would be too skinny to take his weight, but many together might be strong enough to make a bridge. On Joe's side they rested on the ledge. On the other side he manoeuvred them into a crevice between two boulders, which was as close

NO INK CAMP

as he could get to where the wolf had sat. He cut a bit off his precious coil of rope and tied the trunks together on his side so they wouldn't splay out. There were seven saplings altogether. He couldn't tie the far side, but they were firmly wedged together between the rocks. Carrot watched him knot the rope, then she flew to the other side of the river and hopped along a boulder.

Success or a watery death. There was no way of testing the bridge—he'd just have to try it. The water boomed ferociously below him as he crept out onto the bundle of trunks on his hands and knees. The bark was already soaked, and slippery, and hard to grip as he inched along. His arms and chest were saturated and he could barely see for spray. One hand, one knee, other hand, other knee.

He knelt on something sharp and pain shot down his leg. His whole body wobbled. He'd banged that knee when he fell and it had only just stopped hurting; now it was agony. He made himself move again.

The wood under his right hand bent, and cracked; he shifted his weight off it just as the sapling gave way, and grabbed for

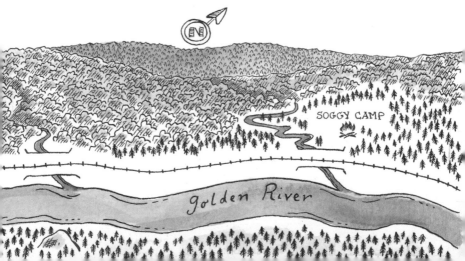

SOGGY CAMP

golden River

another trunk. He tried to crawl faster but his hand slipped forward and he nose-dived onto bark. *More haste, less speed* said his father's voice. *Carefully.* Then his foot was pushing off a slippery rock, his hand grasping for a root, a branch, and he was hauling himself, shaking, on to the safety of the wolf's hidden path.

He found the others in the middle of the day. They'd stopped when the silks ran out and lit a big fire so he could see the smoke. They had saved him his share of the stew.

"Francie kept showing us that you were all right, last night," said Sal. "But she woke up this morning, crying and sweaty—she'd had a terrible dream. Show him, Francie."

Francie showed him two pencil drawings. There was Joe with his curly hair sitting on a raft on a river, but in the second picture Joe was hanging under the raft with his hair floating all around like seaweed.

Joe swallowed his mouthful. "Were you frightened for long?"

She waved her hand. No. And showed him the next page: there was Joe crawling across a bridge made of saplings.

"Amazing!" Did she just know that's how he'd do it? Or was it her idea to make a bridge like that and she'd somehow sent him the thought? Sometimes Joe wondered whether he and Francie really were two separate people. Mostly, he hoped they were.

"Those men are evil. I can't believe they'd strand you like that. They knew we had nothing to do with their stupid keys," Beckett said, not for the first time. "We need to watch out."

When they started up again, Humph trailed behind. He hadn't said anything to Joe.

"What's the matter, Humpty-Dumpty?"

"He's sulking," said Sal, "because I shouted at him. We had a disaster." Sal bent to lift the altimeter over a fern. "Humphrey? Tell Joe."

Humphrey sidled up to Joe. "I'm glad you aren't dead."

"Me too. So what happened?"

"My foot had an accident. And the ink all tipped out. AND I SAID SORRY."

He glared at Sal and raced off.

"Now we have no ink, so Francie can't finish the maps. So this expedition is probably pointless, unless we somehow manage to finish first."

171

"Oh." Joe tried to think of a way in which this might not be a total disaster. "Maybe we can give them pencil maps and promise to finish them later?"

"Hah. Maybe we can make some ink with buckleberries?"

"Yes! Maybe we can," said Joe.

Sal gave him a withering look. "I was being sarcastic."

Sunset was noticeably earlier now, and sunrise later. When they made camp that night it was already dark. Joe lit the lantern so that Francie could draw, in pencil, and Beckett could see to cook.

Humph licked his fingers. "I used to hate mushrooms. Now they're my best."

"Six days to go," said Sal. "How many dinners have we got left, Beckett?"

"Three. And enough pugnut butter for one more lunch." He looked around the forest floor, which was thick with leaves and pine needles. "We'll all have to collect stones in the morning, for the catapult. Tomorrow I really, really need to kill something."

They made good progress the next day as a grassy bank ran above the river, almost like a road, surely perfect for a railway line. Sal groaned when she noticed broken branches, trampled bushes, and footprints in muddy patches.

"Look. Everyone's coming this way. Our route won't be anything special, and they're ahead of us."

Joe refused to be downcast. "But our maps are the best—even if they aren't all in ink. Why don't you ever think about the good things, instead of just the bad ones?"

"Because I'm preparing myself not to be disappointed. Why are you such a ridiculous optimist?"

"Because everything seems to work out in the end. In the last few days I've nearly drowned, I've fallen down a cliff and been stranded in a gorge, but I'm still here. Everything's all right."

"Apart from being hungry."

That was true. His stomach hurt. "Apart from that."

"And having sore feet."

His feet *were* sore but not as sore as his knee. "And that."

Sal shivered. "And now it's getting cold."

"Then put your jacket on."

The temperature was plummeting. They all pulled their extra layers out of their rucksacks. Sal's arms were already in her jumper but her head was still outside when she noticed a dense black cloud billowing over the mountains and rushing to fill the sky.

"Quick! Joe, Francie, the tarpaulin, shelter! Humph—with me, dry wood. Quick. Beckett—water."

No one argued. They scrambled further up the bank and under the trees and got to work. Beckett squinted at the river already dimpled with rain. Then he stripped off all his clothes except his underpants and snatched up the fishing rod and bucket. He looked like a wild two-toned animal as he ran towards the water, with his paper-white back and legs, and dark brown arms, neck and face.

Joe and Francie rigged up a tent by tying one end of the rope to a tree, and the other to a bush that was growing out of a wall of rock. They threw the biggest tarpaulin over the rope, then stretched out the sides, and weighted its edges with stones, spreading the other tarpaulin under. The rain was pelting down by the time they all squashed onto the groundsheet with everything that needed to stay dry. The roof was just above their heads and there was only room for one person to move at a time. Sal crouched near the edge of the shelter, trying to coax a fire out of the wet wood, and coughing with the choking smoke. Carrot perched on Joe's shoulder but kept flapping.

"Stop it! There's no room for wings in here."

"Stop it this minute!" Carrot squawked. "Stop it, stop it, stop it."

Joe cheered when Beckett stumbled up carrying five fat fish and the bucket full of water, but stopped cheering when he realised that Beckett's fingers and lips were blue and he was shivering so violently he couldn't speak.

He took the bucket out of Beckett's bloodless hands and Sal grabbed the fish, and between them they folded him up and squashed him into the shelter. Joe rubbed him with a dryish shirt, then pushed Beckett's arms into his singlet, shirt, jersey and overcoat and coaxed his hands into gloves. Sal pulled her own woolly hat with earflaps over Beckett's head and Joe uncurled Beckett's legs enough to get socks onto his feet and shove his legs into his sleeping bag. The billy boiled and they helped him hold a warm mug of tea in his shaking hands.

When Beckett's teeth stopped chattering enough to talk, he told Francie how to wrap the fish in wet leaves and put them in the hot coals to cook.

Joe breathed in the smell as he unwrapped his neat leaf parcel. "Oh, fantabulous fish. Fine fish. First prize fish. I thought you were going to make us eat seagull."

"I'm so glad you brought the fishing rod," said Sal. "Are you warm now?"

Beckett nodded.

"I didn't used to like fish, but now I do," said Humph when he'd picked every last flake from the skeleton in his bowl. "Fish *and* mushrooms. And look—I've made an H with the bones."

"Only five days left to go," said Sal.

Joe was exhausted, but his knee throbbed and he couldn't get to sleep. Ma had told them never to touch the canvas when it was raining, because the rain would leak straight through. But the night was pitch black and he couldn't see where the side of the tarpaulin sagged down next to him, so he lay still, and concentrated on not rolling over. He listened to the rain pouring off the tarpaulin into the overflowing bucket outside, and the wind bashing branches together, and the miserable sniffling of the sad, wet donkeys, for a very long time.

They woke soaking wet and very cold. A new stream had decided that the quickest way downhill was directly through their shelter, and seemed to be exploring the possibility of growing into a pond. The rain had stopped but the air was damp and water dripped from the leaves and branches overhead. They pulled their rain capes on.

"Keep up, dawdlers," Carrot ordered from Beckett's shoulder.

"Next time I come this way, I'll be in a train," said Beckett, sploshing through yet another stream. "Did you know that some trains have bedrooms in them, Humphrey?"

Humph shook his head. "No. We came on a train. There were only seats and a sliding door. But it could climb."

"The really grand trains have sleeping cars. Little bedrooms with beds with soft mattresses and clean sheets. And your own washbasin. An attendant comes and fills it with hot water. And there's a dining room with tables and chairs, and every table has a cloth on it and a lamp hanging above it, and the best silver cutlery."

"And you'll cook the dinner."

"I will! You can come on the train if you like."

"Let's all come!" said Humphrey. "What will train dinner be?"

"Ham and baked potatoes," suggested Sal.

"Leek and potato soup, and then lamb chops," Joe said. "And Francie wants strawberries." Francie nodded.

"What about me? What about what I want?"

"What do you want, Humph?"

"Ice cream and Christmas cake and peppermint creams and chewy toffee and Ma's fudge."

"Sounds good." Joe took Humph's hand and jumped him over a puddle.

"And white bread toast with butter and honey."

"The best breakfast there is."

When Beckett spotted a pugnut tree they all diverted into the forest to look for nuts, so they were well hidden when a member of Monty's Mountaineers jogged along the riverbank, rain-wet hair plastered to his head.

"That's the one who had a monocle," Joe whispered. "D'you think it was him who stranded me on that ledge?"

Then a few minutes later they saw the one called Gervais puff past in pursuit.

"Or could have been him."

Much later, when the rain had stopped and the bucket was half full of nuts, another of Monty's men limped by, and some way behind him, another, also limping.

They waited, but there was no sign of Baldy.

Not long after that, they climbed over a spur and saw two mechanical horses lying with their hooves in the air at the bottom of a gully. Gervais and Monocle-Man were below them, clambering down towards the wrecked horses.

"That's quite sad," said Joe. "They were so beautiful. I wonder what happened to their riders."

"That's at least seven of Monty's men who've parted company with their horses," said Beckett thoughtfully. "That's a fair number. Some teams will do anything to make sure they win, regardless. And some of them aren't very far away."

CHAPTER NINETEEN

A BOOT
UNDER A BUSH

Sal hoped their camp was far enough into the forest that their fire
wouldn't be seen. She left the others cracking nuts and followed
the stream down to the river. She walked along the river bank
looking and listening, and sniffing the air because she could
smell smoke. Which team was it? And where were they?

It was nearly dark and she was about to turn back when
she heard voices singing, up the hill under the trees. She crept

towards them. Cody Cole and the Cowboys were sitting around their campfire singing a song about being careful not to love anyone because love only ties you down. She hid behind a tree. When the song finished they stood up and stretched.

"Four days to go, men," said Cody Cole. The flames lit their faces from below, making them look ferocious and ghoulish.

"No stopping the Cowboys," said one.

"Whatever it takes," said another.

"Victory at any cost, boys. All together now," said Cody. They put their right hands into a stack. "Victory at any cost."

"Cowboy victory!" they called together and raised their fists into the air.

Sal shivered. When the men had all settled down on their bedrolls she stole away but was startled to hear more voices whispering in front of her. She stopped, but something was breathing right beside her. Then a quiet whinny. She had nearly bumped into a Cowboy's horse.

A twig cracked. A horse? No. The whispering people were now just behind her. The only safe place was up, so she felt for a

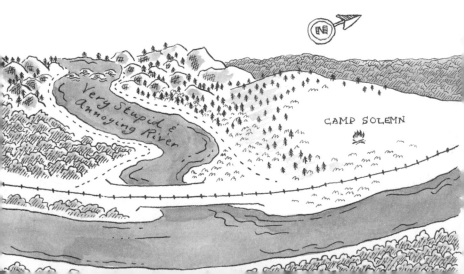

branch and pulled herself into a tree. She pressed herself against the trunk and breathed again. She'd had a lot of experience of hiding in trees when Pa or Ma called her and she wanted to be left alone to read or think; for some reason, when adults are looking for someone they almost never look upwards.

The whispering men came right underneath her. There were three of them; one had a shuttered lantern. They reeked of tobacco. Monty's Mountaineers. Her first thought was that they were planning to hurt the horses. But no. They fussed around untying the horses' tethers and hissing at each other. Then they led the horses quietly away.

Sal waited a few minutes and slid down. It was completely dark and she hadn't a clue how to get back to the others. Out of the trees and towards the river—but which way was that?

As soon as she'd stumbled a safe distance from the Cowboys' camp, Sal paused and ran her fingers over some tree trunks. The side the moss was growing on was north—towards the sea. Soon the slope helped too; the right way was down. After that she heard the river. Then she was out from under the trees and there was a little light from the stars and the moon to help her find her way back along the river bank.

She was just wondering how on earth she'd know which of the many little streams she was crossing was the one that led up to their campsite in the forest when she heard a whistle, and Joe popped up from behind a bush.

"Beckett went up and down the river looking for you. And Humph cried," he said.

Sal was very sorry that the others had been worried. "Thanks for waiting for me." She held onto the hem of his jersey and let him lead her under the dark trees to the glow of their fire. "Is there any dinner left?"

Humph was asleep, but Beckett put another log on the fire and Francie's anxious face shone out of the darkness. Sal thought Beckett was going to snap at her but he just looked relieved and passed her a bowl of cold rice with nuts and wild sorrel chopped into it, which she wolfed down. And in between mouthfuls she told them what she'd seen and heard, and they listened with growing excitement.

Joe nudged Beckett. "We can still be first! We might not have the best maps if they mind about pencil but we can win!"

"Maybe." Beckett nodded slowly. "If the Cowboys waste time fighting with Monty's men, we might be able to overtake both of them. Tortoise and hare. I wonder where the Solemns and the Women Explorers are?"

"Four days to go," said Sal.

They hadn't gone far the next morning when they heard a gunshot. They looked at each other and dragged the donkeys further under the trees.

"They could have been shooting a pigeon for dinner. Or a rabbit," suggested Joe. He hoped they were.

"I don't care if they shoot each other, just so long as no one sees us and decides to sabotage us again," said Beckett. "We've got to be the invisible tortoises."

"What is a tortoise?" asked Humphrey.

"Shh—" said Sal.

A horse and rider pounded along the riverbank, quickly followed by another. The second rider slowed, raised a revolver, fired at the first man then galloped after him.

Joe ran to see. "He got away!"

"That was a Cowboy with the revolver," said Beckett, "so they've got at least one horse back."

They came to a river that flowed into the Golden River—a tributary too wide and fast-flowing to cross, so they had to follow it upstream. It was frustrating to be going in the wrong direction and uphill again. Joe kept scrambling down the bank to see if he could see a crossing place but the river was running through a gorge.

Sal took bearings from a hill on the other side. "The railway can go straight over here but we might have to go hours round. So annoying."

Humph threw a stone down the hill. "I'm going to call it 'Very Stupid and Annoying River'."

"Let's hope it turns out to be too short to write its whole name on the map," said Joe.

"It is," said a voice. "Only a few minutes further to a crossing place."

It was Agatha Amersham. And there were the other members of the Association of Women Explorers. Their camp was colourful, with a row of stripy stockings hanging like flags from a line strung between their two small tents. One woman was sitting on a blanket with a bandaged foot stretched out in front of her. Another was brushing their horse, whose leg was also bandaged, and the fourth one was tending the fire under a steaming billy. She looked up at the new arrivals.

"Good heavens, it's the children!" She left the fire and crossed the grass to peer short-sightedly at them through her glasses. "Well done, well done. Sit down, rest your legs. My goodness, I think this might be a hot chocolate moment, don't you, Agatha?"

"Excellent suggestion," said Agatha. "Mugs out, everyone."

There really was hot chocolate. The short-sighted woman, called Daphne, broke a wedge of chocolate into each cup and topped it with hot water and white powder, which she explained was dried milk.

Joe had never drunk hot chocolate before. It was glorious. He tried to sip it slowly to make it last.

"This is my best ever, ever, ever," said Humph, grinning under a chocolate moustache.

Beckett asked what had happened to their horse and whether it was badly injured.

Agatha frowned. "Someone, we know not who, hurt our beloved Boudica."

"Two nights ago, someone came into our camp, sliced through her halter and stole Boudica," said Daphne. "We searched and searched and eventually Harriet here found her halfway down that bank with an injured leg. We managed to haul her up but in the process Harriet fell and sprained her ankle badly."

"Idiotic thing to do," said Harriet.

"Heroic," said Agatha. "If you hadn't risked your life we'd never have got Boudica out alive, would we, Zinnia?"

"Boudica will recover," said Zinnia, "but it will be a couple of weeks before she can walk far. Nothing to be done but make a comfortable camp and wait."

"That's terrible," said Sal, and told the women about the war between the Cowboys and Sir Monty's team.

"So it's Monty's team who are the horse thieves." Agatha snorted. "I despise people who would allow a defenceless animal to be hurt in order to gain an advantage."

Carrot, who'd been pecking about in the firewood pile, flew onto Agatha's hat and dropped a large green caterpillar onto the brim. Joe tried not to laugh.

Francie rummaged in the first-aid bag and found Ma's pot of salve.

"It's magic," said Humph.

"It really is." Joe held out his hands. "Just a few days ago I fell down a cliff and my hands were pulped. Now look."

He wiggled his fingers to prove they still worked, as they were far too dirty to see any scabs and bruises.

Zinnia took the salve and her eyes welled with tears. "Can you really spare it?"

"Of course we can," said Sal. "It works on humans and horses both. You'll probably be able to walk again tomorrow or the day after, Harriet."

The women said how grateful they were.

Beckett cleared his throat and turned to Agatha. "Excuse me for asking, ma'am, but would you, by any chance, be able to spare us a little ink?"

*

"They were so kind," said Sal as they splashed over the river at the crossing place that Agatha Amersham had shown them. "And they stuck together."

"They could have abandoned Harriet and Boudica and raced on," said Joe. "Cody Cole would have. And Monty."

"I'm going to have hot chocolate every day when I'm rich," said Humph dreamily.

"And we have ink!" said Sal. "That was very clever of you, Beckett."

Beckett's ears turned pink. "Well, there's no harm in asking, is there?"

When they reached the point on the opposite side of the gorge that she'd marked as the place for a bridge across Very Stupid and Annoying River, Sal stopped to measure and Francie inked in the map. Joe and Beckett persuaded Humph to stay with the mapmakers and they went on ahead. Beckett took the bucket, determined to find something to cook for dinner, and Joe took the slasher to clear a path through the undergrowth, which was much thicker on this side of the valley. Except he didn't need to, because they soon came across a ready-made path that was going in exactly the right direction. Beckett thought it must have been trampled by animals—bears perhaps, or wild pigs—though they couldn't see any spoor or scraps of fur on the bark of trees. Joe held the slasher tightly, just in case they met something fierce. Beckett had his catapult and knife at the ready in the hope that the path had been made by a wild boar; he talked of roast pork and described how to make delicious crackling.

Joe noticed a flash of blue. A branch had been pulled back and tied to the one next to it with a blue thread. He untied it and showed it to Beckett.

"Strange. Have you ever seen the like?" asked Beckett.

"Never. It's so strong."

Beckett tried to snap it but he couldn't, even though it was as fine as a hair. "You could wind up a mile of that and still hold the ball in one hand."

A prickle bush had been chopped off at knee height; some person had definitely cut this trail, and that someone was ahead of them. They came to another deliberately tied-up branch, and another.

"It's got to be the Solemn men," Joe said. "That thread is totally scientific. And it must mean that at least some of the Solemn men are behind us. Brilliant!" said Joe.

"Except maybe the following Solemns have already passed here and just not bothered to untie the threads," said Beckett.

"Oh. That's true," said Joe sadly. "I think my brain's slowing down because I'm so hungry." The delicious full-up feeling from the hot chocolate had long since worn off.

But at least the track was easy to follow and soon they were walking along the bank of the Golden River again. Late in the afternoon the trees thinned out and they came into a clearing. The sun was bright, but there was a cold wind scouring the valley. Joe shivered and crouched by the water's edge for a drink. He didn't immediately notice the booted foot that stuck out next to some crackerjack vine.

When he did, he nearly fell backwards into the river. He stood up quietly. There was another boot, and both boots were attached to legs, brown-knitted legs, and above that a brown-knitted jersey. And a head. It was one of the Solemn men. Asleep? Or dead?

Joe coughed loudly but the man didn't stir.

He called, "Hello? Hello?" and looked around. Definitely no one else there. He held his breath and crept nearer. He'd never seen a dead person before. He touched the man's hand. It was cold as snow.

Then the man groaned and Joe's heart started thumping again.

"So you're not dead, then? That's good." He squatted down. The man looked like the leader, Keith Skinner, though it was hard to tell as a lot of his face was covered in a new beard and moustache. His face was blue-tinged in the places that weren't deeply tanned, like his eyelids, behind his ears and below the hair on his neck. His eyes opened—even the whites were blue.

Carrot landed on one of the man's boots. "Dearie me."

"Are you hurt? Where's the rest of your team?"

"Nearly there," Skinner mumbled through clenched teeth. "Steak for protein, iron, more hydrogen …"

Joe touched him on the arm. The man's clothes were sopping wet. "Did you fall in the river? I think you've got hypothermia."

There was a slasher lying near Keith Skinner's rucksack. Inside the rucksack was a ball of the blue thread, a scarf, which Joe wrapped round Skinner's head and ears, some chemical-looking jars and packages, a cup and a plate. No food, and no dry clothes.

Joe took off his own jacket and tucked it over Skinner. "Lucky for you the cavalry's coming."

"What have you found?" Beckett came down the river bank, bucket in one hand and a dead pigeon in the other. "It's a Solemn! Is he by himself?"

"Seems to be."

"He can't be lost, surely?"

"Don't know. He's freezing."

They quickly dragged dry wood into a pile and made a fire. When Keith Skinner's lips were less blue, he whispered, "Food."

"Can we spare anything?"

Beckett lowered the bucket. There were eight small eggs in it. "Pigeon's eggs. He can have one, I suppose."

Keith Skinner's eyes were huge in his bony face. He grabbed an egg, broke it into his mouth and swallowed it raw.

CHAPTER TWENTY

THE SCUMBAG
CRUMB-BAG

It wasn't until they'd all finished eating their roast pigeon meat with scrambled pigeon eggs and rice that Keith Skinner deigned to talk.

The first thing Joe wanted to know was, "What happened to your magic clouds?"

Skinner scowled. "Rain."

"And where's the rest of your team?" asked Sal.

He jerked his head towards the mountains, looked round

uneasily and didn't say anything. He finished his cup of tea and held it out to Beckett for a refill.

Humphrey poked Skinner's leg. "What happened to your friends? You got to tell."

"Fever."

"Fever?" Sal jumped up and lifted Humph further away from Skinner. "You mean they're sick? Are you sick, too? I thought you were just starving."

Skinner's eyes flashed. "*Gold* fever. They found a fist-sized nugget. Then they lost it. But they found some evidence of ore in the river on the other side of Skinner's Pass and they refused to continue."

"Skinner's Pass? I don't think so," said Beckett.

"They are suffering from an addiction," Skinner sneered. It was clear he didn't think much of such unscientific behaviour.

"But what about your magic clouds?" said Joe.

"The nebulism failed when we experienced precipitation. Plotkin's fault. Bags were insufficiently waterproofed. Consequence was, we were forced to carry our provisions. In order to expedite our progress, I ordered my men to abandon some of

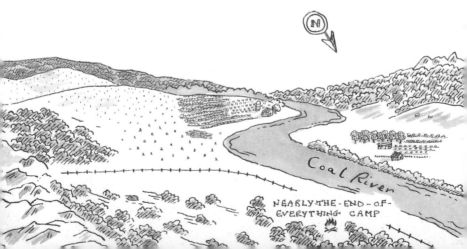

Coal River

NEARLY-THE-END-OF-
EVERYTHING CAMP

the weight, and gave Sanchez responsibility for rearranging the loads. His decision-making was faulty and the outcome was an inadequately nutritious calorific supply."

"Which I think is science talk for 'the clouds got wet and stopped floating so they had to leave stuff behind and they didn't take enough food'," Sal explained to Humph.

Keith Skinner glared at her. "Then Buxton, my draftsman, failed to secure the seal on the map cylinder with the consequence that when I became briefly submerged crossing the River Keith, the contents were rendered indecipherable."

Humph looked at Sal.

"The maps got wet and too soggy to read," she translated.

"Then Cranshaw thought he found a streak. Started hunting. Plotkin found a nugget. Determined to stay there, do geological survey, mine gold." He narrowed his eyes and glared at a point in the distance as if he could see his men there, and snarled bitterly as though they could hear him. "They considered the odds of success likely to be more profitable; without maps, there was no longer any possibility of winning anything but 'first team back' and we'd been so delayed they assumed other teams to be ahead of us. They promised they would follow me, so I went ahead to cut the trail. But it appears they were lying."

Joe felt a bubble of excitement growing inside him. "You mean your team has stopped racing? We might be in the lead?"

"I doubt it," Skinner snapped. "I observed that Sir Monty has abandoned many of his mechanical horses, but his men are experienced mountaineers and will have been making rapid advances, and Cody Cole's Cowboys will undoubtedly be progressing at maximum velocity. Their horses are muscular and they have sufficient manpower to maintain a system of scouts. They never have to retrace their steps." He spat on the ground. "The women's team have abandoned the race, and Roger Rumpledown is more interested in the brandy that comprises the bulk of his supplies. No. Cody Cole will win. Or possibly Sir Monty."

"We'll see," said Beckett. "Still three days to go."

In the morning, Keith Skinner watched Beckett smother the fire and Sal tie the donkeys' baskets on.

"Are you coming with us now?" asked Joe.

"Maybe," said Skinner. He looked shifty.

"Stay there a minute," said Joe. He went into a huddle with the others, except Humphrey who was practising somersaults.

"I don't trust him," said Sal.

"Whatever happens he mustn't see you drawing, Francie," Beckett said. "And keep tight hold of the maps."

Francie nodded. Joe could see that she was worried. She didn't trust Skinner any more than Sal did.

They decided that Skinner should go ahead with Joe.

"It's a trial," Sal told him fiercely. "If you are any kind of trouble, we won't share our food."

With Skinner helping Joe cut the path, they travelled fast. Skinner said that he thought New Coalhaven was only a day or two away. And then they came to a bend in the river. Instead of going straight to the ocean, it turned to the east; if they stayed next to it, it could take them miles in the wrong direction.

"I don't believe it—I thought we were so close!" Joe hurled a stone into the water.

He beckoned to Sal and Francie and spoke very quietly. "We should probably go over the hill there, not keep following the river. But I don't know. And you can't fly with him around, Francie." He jerked his head towards Skinner. "I need to see where we're going though. I'm going to climb up to that lookout."

Sal nodded. "See if you can take him with you, then Francie can work on the maps."

"I think I'll go up there, by myself, and see how far we've got to go," Joe announced, pointing up the hill to a rocky outcrop above the trees.

"I'll come, too," said Skinner, as Joe guessed he would.

"Come on then," he said, trying to sound reluctant.

He exchanged a secret smile with Francie. Some people were so easy to trick.

It was hot work going up the hill, but Skinner kept up and in half an hour they were out in the open again and clambering over the last rocks to a brilliant 360-degree lookout.

Their journey was nearly over. There was the gleaming sea, and the haze of the chimneys of New Coalhaven. There were farmhouses in the distance, and what looked like a village. Civilisation! In the valley ahead, some of the forest had been cleared, and those white dots were surely sheep. Joe looked across the valley; there on the opposite ridge, not half a mile away, was a man on horseback, a man wearing a Stetson hat. Something flashed near the man's face—sunlight on a lens. A uniscope, perhaps, directed straight at Joe and Skinner. Then the watcher turned his horse and galloped away towards a line of horses in the far distance. Cody Cole and his Cowboys must have rescued all their horses from the thieving Mountaineers. And they were behind the Santanders.

"He saw us, but we're ahead by at least an hour, maybe two. Come on!" Joe leapt off the rock and down the hill, but Skinner didn't follow. Joe yelled at him to hurry, but when he still didn't appear, he climbed back up to the lookout, expecting to see Skinner holding a twisted ankle. But there was no sign of him. Then Joe saw a figure hurtling downhill on the other side of the spur, leaping over bushes and rocks, heading for the coast.

Joe cursed him as he ran down the hill.

"It's not far to go," he shouted to the others, "but you'll never guess what that man did! He let us save his life and then he raced off the minute he saw a chance to get ahead." He saw Sal's face and stopped. "What is it?"

"He's stolen the oats and the raisin jar, and today's bread," said Beckett.

"One pudding left," Sal said. "He didn't see that. We'll just have to go as fast as we can tomorrow and beat him."

"What a scumbag!" said Joe.

"What a crumb-bag!" said Humph.

They urged the donkeys on and didn't stop until it was so dark they couldn't see their feet.

There were only two more days to go.

*

Something woke Joe. He'd been dreaming of drumming hoof beats. It was still dark, but there was a glow from the fire and the first light of very early morning. As he was trying to get comfortable he noticed that the shape that should have been next to him wasn't there. No Humphrey? Probably cuddled up with Francie. He was nearly asleep again when something in his brain made him sit up and squint at the other sleeping-bag bumps. Humphrey wasn't cuddled up with Francie. Nor with Sal, nor with Beckett.

Peeing? He called out softly and when there was no answer he wriggled out of his sleeping bag. He crept round the designated pee bush—no Humph. Over to where the donkeys were sleeping—no Humph.

"Humph? Humphrey? Where are you?" He was panicking now and called louder.

The others stumbled out of their sleeping bags.

"But where…?"

"He can't have gone far."

"Sleep-walking?"

Sleep-walking! Joe ran to the river; in the grey light it was pale stones with a channel of black water on the far side. Humph had gone to sleep in his red jersey. Joe scanned the stones for anything red, but there was no colour anywhere.

CHAPTER TWENTY-ONE

DESPERATION
AND DESPAIR

"Humph?" Joe called. "Humph!"

They blundered about in the dark, calling in voices that became more and more desperate. Sal lit the lantern and crawled under bushes while Beckett searched the track to the river.

Joe found a candle stub. "Are you hiding? Come out, this isn't funny." But he knew Humph wasn't hiding—he liked his

NEARLY-THE-END-OF-
EVERYTHING CAMP

Coal River

sleep too much. The blood was thumping in his ears so loudly that he could barely hear his own voice screaming. "Humph! Humphrey?"

This was the worst fear of all.

Francie was scouring the edge of the clearing, bending, peering, feeling into dark spaces, when she straightened up and beckoned Joe urgently. She took his candle and showed him a patch of trampled grass. Had they done that? Sal ran over and held up the lantern. Past the trampled grass was some mud with the clear outline of a horseshoe impressed into it.

Beckett came running when Sal yelled. He took the lantern and peered at a branch. "A horse was tethered here. The bark's been scraped off. And not long ago, because this dung's still warm."

"You mean—" Joe thought he was going to throw up.

"He's been stolen," said Sal, collapsing against a tree.

"Cody Cole," Joe whispered, as if the Cowboy might be listening. "His scout saw me."

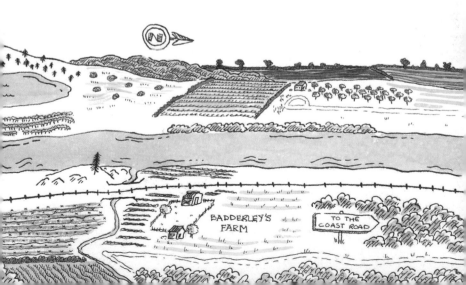

"Follow the hoof prints, quick." Beckett held the lantern up and Francie scouted for the next print and the next.

"If they hurt him …" Sal and Joe snatched up strong sticks as they ran.

They followed the trail to an open hillside. It was lighter here; the sun was rising. Which way had the horse gone? They ran in every direction but couldn't find any marks on the short grass.

Sal's eyes were huge and her voice was panicky. "He mustn't get away!"

"Which way? Which way?"

Francie lay down and prepared to fly.

Low trees leaning into the hill; nowhere to hide a horse. Around the hill, up a little, round again, up. Where is he? Where is he? Sun rise. Bright light, long shadows. North first, where mist's floating over fields, fences, farmhouses.

Red jersey. Red jersey. Looking for a red jersey. Red? No just a bush. Red? No—washing on a line. Red? No, a barn door.

Strange shapes on the eastern hills, Castles? Closer. Not castles. Giant chimneys. Huge, clanking wheels hanging from towers, and people walking to work. No horse, no rider, no red, no Humphrey.

Turn south and west. No buildings, just forest and open moorland on hilltops. Nothing moving except morning birds and a lonely goat.

But there! It's the Cowboys, by a small lake. Loading their

horses. Cody Cole, already in the saddle, and one, two, three, four—five other men. No Humphrey, and one man and one horse missing.

As soon as he saw Francie's face, Joe knew it wasn't good. She drew the Cowboys on their horses and a sketch-map that showed where they were, and which direction they were going in.

"Six. There's a horse missing?"

Francie nodded and carried on drawing. She put the sun going down—and showed the horsemen in New Coalhaven.

"So Cody Cole will get to New Coalhaven tonight, and—" Sal broke off as Beckett ran towards them, shouting.

"Over there! I've found where the horse went into the trees."

The signs were a little way into the forest. Some snapped-off twigs, a hoof print. Further on, some more dung. The trail was easy to follow until they came to a shallow stream where it seemed to vanish.

Francie said she'd fly again, even though she was trembling and had grey shadows around her eyes. She hadn't flown twice in one day before.

"What happens if you don't sleep after flying?" Joe had never felt so much worry piling in on him. "Promise you'll come back and rest before you get too tired?"

She nodded. He made her come with him to their camp, drink some water and put her socks on. She really needed to eat but there was no food left, nothing. He cracked three

pugnuts that he'd been saving in his pocket and gave them to her, and the last mouthful of Doctor Sopworth's Restorative Tonic from Ma's lotions and potions bag, then they went back to the open hillside.

"You'll find him. I know you will." He hugged her.

Round and round in widening cirles. Everything is green and brown and black shadow. Red? red? No red. *Where are you, little Humph?* Where?

And then—

And then he's there.

That way. Down through the trees, this is hard. A hidden path. A horse, a cave, too dark to see properly. *Humphrey?*

Yes! Francie, Francie!

I'm here.

It's a crack in the rock, a tiny space. The Cowboy's sprawled asleep, boots sticking out of the entrance and his head on his arm. Behind him, Humph tied with a rope around wrists and ankles.

He can't move.

But there's a knife. Think a picture. *Knife, Humph, knife! Under the loaf of bread on the Cowboy's pack.*

Now he's seen it. It's out of reach. He wriggles.

Sore elbows, sore knees! But he's nearly there. He kneels up, reaches out, lifts the bread. He's about to pick up the knife when the guard stirs. Humph freezes.

The guard yawns, stretches. Arm out, his hand's about to discover Humph—but instead of Humph, his hand finds the bread, which Humph's holding out to him. His fingers close around it. He rolls over and falls back to sleep cuddling the loaf to his leather waistcoat.

Humph's fingers curl around the handle of the knife.

But the Cowboy guard has stretched sideways, so now one booted leg blocks the exit —blocks Humph's escape.

He shuffles forward on his knees until he's close by the Cowboy's leg.

How will he ever get past?

There is a way. Think the picture for him. *Somersault Humph!*

Humph struggles to his feet, then silently lowers his hands still holding the knife, until they reach the ground beyond the leg, his body a bridge. The rope between wrist and ankle lies across the cowboy's boot. Humph shuffles his feet a little closer in. And his hands.

Head in.

He pushes off and somersaults clear over the guard's leg and into the open, knife still clasped between his hands.

Best somersault ever! He rolls away.

Yay! Now, knife on rope, saw, saw.

Humph is surprised. *But the knife's sharp. Should I?*

Humph saws, tongue sticks out between his teeth.

His arms are tired. Holds the knife still and moves his feet.

The cord gives way. Humph's legs are free; he can stand and run. His hands are small, the rope is slack, he slips one out, then both. He's up and off, racing down the green path.

Must tell … so tired … others. Need … join myself. First, find place, you hide.

Humph runs, then walks, then runs. He drinks at a stream then hurries on.

Up through the air above treetops. Where are they? Over the forested hills to the southwest. Her body signals like a magnetic pulse.

Downhill, farmland. Fields, farmhouse. Another roof. A barn for Humph to hide in. So tired, him too. Hold onto the picture of where he is. Hold onto the picture of the way the others must go to find him.

Down to main river, downstream to lone pine on a hillock, then up small stream east past farm with red roof, to barn in the corner of paddock.

Humph lifts the latch and drags the door open; the air's thick and grassy. Hay's piled up for winter, but no animals there, no reason anyone will come. Humph makes a nest and sucks his thumb.

Love you, Humph.

Up, up, but it's too hard. Fading, fading. Up a little, then a little more. Pink and green clouds are streaked across the deepening blue. Dusk already? The ground is blurred. Fades. Disappears.

Downstream. Lone pine, up ... Past farm red roof. Barn.

Down, down, pine, red, barn ...

CHAPTER TWENTY-TWO

TIME SUSPENDED

Francie didn't move. Joe put his face close to her nose and felt the faintest wisp of breath on his cheek.

"Keep breathing, Francie." He straightened the tarpaulin that he'd pulled over her sleeping bag to protect it from the dew, then dragged the last branch onto the fire. Sparks flew up into the early morning sky. Beyond the fire he could make out the silhouettes of trees against the dawn horizon, and hear Treacle grazing.

He stood up and stretched, sat down, then stood up again. When Francie had returned to her body, her skin had been so pale it was almost transparent, like frogspawn, and her hand had trembled so much she could hardly hold the pencil. Joe had wrapped everything warm he could find round her—he'd been so frightened he'd started shaking too.

He felt Francie's neck. Definitely warm. Maybe too warm?

She'd drawn a map that was as basic as something Humphrey would draw. It showed a river and a couple of streams, a hill, a tree and a barn with a stick figure in it, and then she'd started retching, and her eyes had rolled back in her head and she'd become unconscious. Joe's stomach scrunched up when he thought about it—and he couldn't stop thinking about it. Every time he closed his eyes he saw Francie faint again. Best stay awake, stay on guard. Think about something else.

It was over twenty-four hours now since Humph had gone missing and longer than that since Joe had eaten anything. His tummy rumbled and growled. That was something else not to think about.

"I'm not thinking about food. Not thinking about cake. Not thinking about baked potatoes or bread. Not even thinking about porridge." He put a blade of grass between his teeth to have something to nibble on, and turned around to warm his back.

When his back was toasty he wandered over to where the donkeys' loads were piled up. When they'd first set off, the loads had been tidy and they'd known where everything was. Now it was a jumble. The pile was a lot smaller than at the beginning of the journey, and the difference wasn't just the food they'd eaten. Joe only had three socks left in all the world: the brown and the blue one he was wearing, plus a stripy one with a hole in the heel. But three socks were enough, when you thought about it.

He up-ended the panniers and emptied the sacks. Ma and Pa had drilled into them that they must always be vigilant with the surveying and map-making tools and the paper and pens, and they had been; all those things were still in their cases and water-proof tubes. They'd managed to leave the spade somewhere, but Joe found the axe, which he'd looked for yesterday, all tangled up in the empty rice sack. And they still had quite a lot of rope.

He smoothed the sack out. It had a lump in it. An apple? No. Sal's gloves.

They'd abandoned the water barrel after it started to leak, and none of them had seen the uniscope for days, but they still had the billy and the cooking pot, and a couple of knives and spoons, and some mugs and bowls.

A birdcall startled him. It was almost daybreak. Soon there was a cacophony of bird noise; it was hard to believe that this racket went on every morning and he usually slept through it. The birds woke Carrot, and she flew into the trees towards a call that sounded like "bis-cuit, bis-cuit". Joe's stomach growled and grumbled and he tried to remember how many days Pa and Ma had gone without food when they got stuck in a blizzard at Crater Lake. It was more than two.

Why weren't they here now?

He shook the rest of the sacks out, just in case there was a miraculous lost cheese or a packet of dried plums they never knew they had. But the only surprising thing was a tent peg. He put it in the bucket. At least they hadn't lost the bucket.

He thought he heard a noise and ran back to Francie; she hadn't moved but was still breathing. He poked the fire, then loaded everything back into the donkeys' baskets so it was shipshape and ready to go. The birds finished their morning chorus and the day grew quiet. The sun crept down the hill until it reached him, and bees followed it, buzzing round the meadow clover.

Now what? He practised some bear-scaring moves with his fire-poking stick, but then the stick broke.

What could he do? If there was a cow or a goat nearby he could milk it. But there wasn't. He went to talk to Treacle, but he was sulking and turned and showed him his tail.

"Be like that, then. I thought you'd be pleased to have a rest. Dumpling's just gone down the valley with Sal and Beckett to find Humph, then they're walking back up here. It's just more work for Dumpling. She's not getting special food or anything." Treacle didn't listen.

"Come on, Sal, Beckett, Humph. It's morning now. Come on." How far away was that barn? How much longer could they possibly be?

He crouched over Francie and tried wishing her to wake up: *please, please, please.* He unpacked one of her hands from its covers and squeezed it gently, but she didn't respond.

What if Sal and Beckett had met Cody Cole and his Cowboys? What if they'd found Humph but he'd been really well guarded? What if the Cowboys had kidnapped them, too? Or they'd had to fight? Maybe he should have gone, but he couldn't leave Francie. She needed him; she didn't need Sal or Beckett, not in the same way. And now they'd been gone all night.

Joe had never been awake all night before. He felt as if he had wind-up clockwork inside him, and all he could do was listen for Francie's breathing and for the others coming up the hill. Maybe they'd got lost in the dark. Maybe they hadn't found Humphrey. Maybe they'd never come back. Maybe Francie would never wake up. Maybe he was all alone in the world now. No Ma, no Pa, no Sal or Humph ...

A crow swooped past. One for sorrow. Or was that magpies?

The fire was burning down. He made himself go up the slope to the edge of the forest to look for more wood. There was a dead tree lying collapsed on the ground and as he went to pick up some branches he heard a loud buzzing. Hundreds of bees were flying in and out of a hole in the trunk. It was like a jolt of lightning in his brain.

Honey!

He raced back to the baskets and threw everything out again. When he'd helped move the bee woman's hives, she'd made him wear a special bee-keeper's suit and a hat with a veil to keep the bees off his face. He put on Humph's sou'wester hat and pulled Humph's spare jersey over the top so the crown stuck through the head hole and the rest of it hung down over the hat brim like a veil. He could see well enough through the knitting.

He tucked the bottom of the jersey into the neck of his shirt to keep the bees out, pulled on Sal's gloves and put a knife and a spoon into the billy. The bee woman had used a special smoke puffer to make the bees sleepy. He picked a glowing branch out of the fire. It barely smoked, so he threw it back and shovelled some burning embers into the cooking pot instead, then filled it up with leaves and pine needles. They smoked beautifully. He waved the smoking pot around him as he approached the bee tree. The buzzing seemed to become more ferocious as he got nearer, but he tried to stay calm because he knew bees could smell fear. He spoke softly to them.

"Please don't sting me. I only want a little bit of your honey for my sister who needs it, and I won't hurt you."

He put the smoking pot on the ground near the hole and pushed it up to the trunk with his foot. The noise of the bees quietened and they moved more slowly. There were bees on his trousers now, and several crawling on the jersey in front of his face.

"Nice bees, good bees," he murmured.

He leaned over the hole. He could see a big slab of honeycomb in there, and what looked like thousands more bees.

It would have been easier with more hands. He stuck the billycan between his knees and took the knife out. Slowly, slowly he reached forward with the knife in his gloved hand. Bees crawled over the blade as he pushed down on it and sliced off a chunk of the waxy comb, dripping with liquid golden honey. He picked up the spoon, balanced the honeycomb between the spoon and knife, and guided it into the billycan.

"Thank you, bees," he murmured as he backed away slowly. "Thank you very much. Thank you, thank you."

He didn't get stung until he was back by the fire pulling the hat and jersey-veil off. He felt a sharp sting on his ear from a poor bee whose legs must have got trapped in the wool. He tried to ignore it. Francie first. He spooned up some shiny honey and smeared it on her lips, then he pushed the spoon gently into her mouth and tipped the honey onto her tongue. He sat her up so her head was resting on his shoulder, then he scooped some more honey into her mouth and scraped a bit of honeycomb onto her teeth.

"Come on, Francie, come on."

At last he saw her swallow. It was working!

He squeezed her shoulder. "That's it, keep going."

Joe licked his fingers and a trickle of honey slid down his throat.

Heavenly.

A spoonful for Francie and a spoonful for him.

Then Francie moved. Her tongue flicked out round her lips.

"Yes! Good, Francie."

She licked her lips again, and her eyelids fluttered. Her eyes opened.

"You're awake!"

He held a cup of water to Francie's mouth and she drank. Then she opened her mouth again like a baby bird and he popped a spoon of honey in, wax and all. She held the spoon and sucked.

He beamed at her. He'd accidently dribbled honey into

her hair and across her face and there were sticky trails over their clothes, but she was awake! He licked his hands—he was sticky, too.

She looked around at the fire, the hillside, one donkey. And something else. She turned to Joe. In the distance, a deep bass rumbling sound.

CHAPTER TWENTY-THREE

STUMBLING TO THE FINISH LINE

Joe peered down the hill. He could see smoke puffing up in time with a rhythmic clanking but he still couldn't see the machine that was making the terrifying noise. Should he try to drag Francie under the trees? It was coming nearer and nearer.

A red chimney appeared, then a bright red roof. A boiler, huge wheels. It looked a bit like a train engine, chugging relentlessly

Coal River

up the hill, but there were no tracks, and it wasn't pulling carriages, just a cart. There were heads looking over the side of the cart. It was Sal, and Beckett, and Humph waving and waving. The huge red dragon came to a stop.

Joe shouted, "She's woken up! She's all right!" and Sal's anxious face split into a huge grin.

Humph hurtled out of the cart and over to Joe. He seemed to have forgotten his terrifying experience already; he was far more excited by his ride and the fact he was bringing Joe food. The woman driving the engine pulled on lots of levers and climbed down and introduced herself. She was Mrs Baddeley; she'd found Humph in her barn.

She thrust a packet at Joe. A bacon sandwich! The bread was still warm. He bit into its soft buttery deliciousness. Everyone was safe and they even had food.

Francie shook her head at Mrs Baddeley's sandwiches but took another spoonful of honey and stood up without help.

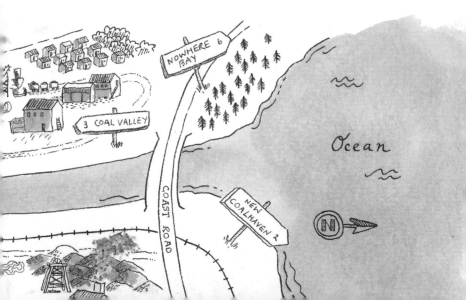

Sal pulled Joe aside. "Mrs Baddeley says we can still make it, if we hurry. Gallop not trot. Do you think Francie can?"

The race! It had gone completely out of his mind. Once Joe would have shouted, "Of course, let's go!" but not now. He'd watched Francie's unconscious face for too long.

"I don't know," he said. "How far is it?"

"Half an hour down to the farmhouse and then six or seven hours' walk to town."

"That's a long way. But Treacle's had a rest. Maybe he can carry Francie?"

Sal nodded. "Let's try." She bellowed at the others: "We're going to New Coalhaven today. Let's gallop!"

Joe and Beckett ran to put out the fire.

"Pee on it, boys," Mrs Baddeley suggested over her shoulder as she and Sal helped Francie into the cart, with the honey bucket.

"Really?" Humph ran to help.

"So what happened?" Joe asked.

"We got to the barn but no Humphrey," said Beckett.

"Mrs Badgey said did I want breakfast and I said yes please and I said you all did too so she got out her biggest frying pan. It's humungous," said Humph. "Then we came in her trac-sher engine. It's strong. Stronger than two horses even!"

"Traction," said Beckett. "Traction engine. They can do anything. Lift, tow, power a thresher or a pump. They are the future."

The fire was out. Joe bent to pick up the basket of tools, but it fell apart.

"Just throw everything in the cart," said Mrs Baddeley.

They dumped the tools next to Francie. She was looking pale

and there were beads of sweat on her face, but she was sucking on the honey spoon and looking about her.

Beckett and Joe ran to get the rucksacks. "When did she wake?"

"Just before you got here. I found some wild honey and it woke her up."

"Did you get stung?"

"Only once."

"The bees must have liked you—or her. Put some honey on it. Stops it hurting so much."

Beckett persuaded Treacle to follow the traction engine down the hill, following Sal who was pulling the altimeter. By the time the procession reached the Baddeley farmyard, Francie looked almost like her normal self.

"It's the honey," said Mrs Baddeley. "Those bees know a thing or two. Smarter than a lot of folks, I reckon."

Mrs Baddeley said to put everything in her shed while she made them more sandwiches and filled their water bottle.

"When you get to New Coalhaven, you ask directions to my sister-in-law's house—the other Mrs Baddeley. She'll give you a bed tonight, she has beds a-plenty. Now get on your way."

But the donkeys had other ideas. They had their noses in the long grass and windfall apples of the orchard and refused to budge. Beckett pulled, Joe pushed, Sal shouted, Humph held apples just out of reach, Mrs Baddeley waved a stick, and Carrot dug her claws into Treacle's head and told him off, but it made no difference. Those donkeys weren't going anywhere.

Francie danced through the trees to show that she was strong enough to go on foot.

"Let's risk it," said Sal.

It felt strange having no donkeys with them as they walked down the lane on the grass strip between two dry wheel ruts. Sal pulled the altimeter. It clicked round steadily, but the worry lines made deep creases in her forehead.

Humphrey told Joe the story of how he'd escaped from the Cowboy. "Francie sent me pictures, to show me. At least, maybe she did. Or maybe I just thought. But I took this really sharp knife and I cut the rope on my legs and I didn't even hurt myself! And I did the best-ever somersault!"

"You are a champion, Humphrey Santander. And everything is all right now, and we're nearly there."

Joe took one of his hands and Francie the other and they swung along together.

"And Ma might be waiting for us," said Sal.

"Prob'ly she'll be there," said Humph.

"Almost certainly," said Sal.

The road ran between fields and woods, and then between black hills with nothing growing on them.

"Mine spoil," said Beckett.

There were noisy towers all the way down the valley. The tallest ones belched black smoke, the square ones were topped with huge, clanking, winding wheels, and a hideous screech came out of the funnel-shaped ones.

They crossed the tramway ahead of an engine hauling a line of empty coal wagons back up the valley. Humph waved to the driver, and he waved back, before being engulfed in a puff of smoke from the engine's chimney. They went past rows of houses all coated with soot. Even the plants in their tiny front gardens were covered in grime. Nothing was green here, nothing shiny.

After being in the wilds for so long Joe felt strange being near people and buildings and man-made noise again. Smaller. Francie's shoulders were hunched up. She felt the same.

"Is this what progress looks like, Beckett?" asked Sal.

Beckett shrugged. "You have to get your power from somewhere, I suppose." He didn't look entirely convinced. "Agreed I wouldn't want to swim in that river—or fish."

"The air smells horrible," said Joe. "And it tastes nasty."

Then Francie stumbled. Joe grabbed her arm to save her from falling. "Sal! Quick!"

Francie's face was drained of colour and she was swaying on her feet. Beckett scooped her up and carried her to a low wall and made her sit with her head between her knees.

"Don't try to get up," Beckett said in a gentle voice.

They passed the water bottle round and had a sandwich, though Francie only managed one mouthful.

"How long until sunset?" Joe asked Sal in a whisper.

Sal squinted up. A yellowish-grey pall covered the sun now. "Can't be sure, maybe two hours?"

Francie got up and started walking again and they hurried after her. At last they came around a bend in the road and the view opened up in front of them. There was the ocean, and the waves rolling in. Through the haze they could see the smoking chimneys of the town, and the smoke stacks of the steamers approaching the port. The shadows were long but the sun was still more than a hand's width above the horizon.

When they came to the junction with the coast road a signpost pointed back the way they'd come: *Coal Valley 3* and *Nowhere Bay 6* to the left, and to the right, *New Coalhaven 2*.

"Only two to go!" Humph shouted.

But Francie was swaying, a pulse throbbing in her temple.

"The map! We've got to finish the map," said Sal. There was a beer house ahead, with a bench seat outside. Joe and Beckett took an elbow each and steered Francie to sit down. She managed to drink a few sips of water, then Joe unrolled the final map and spread it on the bench next to her. Beckett held down the end to stop it rolling up again and Humph held Francie's pens and pencils ready. Sal took the scroll out of the altimeter and stood by to check off heights on the map.

But Francie just sat with her eyes closed. She didn't move.

"We should have brought the rest of the honey," Joe said in a low voice. He went to see if he could get some from the publican, but there was a notice on the door:

GONE TO WATCH RACE—BACK TOMORROW

There were no more buildings nearby. Which way should they go for help? A cloud of dust was approaching along the road from Nowhere Bay, accompanied by a rumble and a screech of metal on metal that was getting louder. It was a mechanical horse clanking along with Sir Monty on its back. The horse's paint was scraped and battered and most of its tail and mane were missing. Sir Monty squinted fiercely, teeth clenched around his pipe, and didn't even seem to notice them as he passed.

The Belgian tracking hound limped along after him, head hanging low, tongue out and panting. Its coat and tail were full of twigs and burrs. Behind it, three of Monty's men were following on bicycles, pedalling madly. They all looked much thinner, hairier and more ragged than when they'd set off.

"Hey, can you help us?" Joe called, but he might as well have been invisible.

"Change!" shouted the leading cyclist when they were opposite the signpost, and all three dropped their bikes at the side of the road and continued on foot.

"Why on earth?" said Joe. "We should take the bikes if they don't want them."

Francie stirred, blinked, saw the map, and nodded. She looked all around and closed her eyes again.

"Come on, Francie," Sal whispered.

Francie seemed to shake herself awake, then slid to the ground. Joe thought she was fainting, but she pulled herself around to face the bench seat as a desk, and took a pen from Humph. Sal unscrewed the lid of the ink pot. Francie's hand was steady as she marked the route down Black Valley, and the road to New Coalhaven, and filled in the final heights and landmarks.

The sun was dropping fast; Joe jiggled with impatience and the others stood ready to move as soon as Francie finished. Another cloud of dust came down the road. It was three more of Monty's men, on foot, looking just as weather-beaten and unkempt as the first lot. They weren't talking to each other, or carrying anything, they just kept their eyes fixed on the distance and mumbled "left, right, left, right". They walked straight past the bicycles.

Sal stared at Humph and Joe as if she'd never seen them before. "You know what? We look even worse than those Mountaineers do. Maybe we ought to wash or something, so people can recognise us?"

They looked as though they'd had birds nesting in their hair; every crease and crevice of their skin was filled with dirt, and their clothes were ripped and so filthy they could have stood up on their own.

"My thumb's clean," said Humph, taking it out of his mouth to show her.

Sal wet Mrs Baddeley's sandwich cloth in the horse-trough that stood by the beer house's hitching rail. She wiped some of the grime off Humph's face and splashed her own face and neck.

"We still look terrible."

Joe ducked away as she threatened to wipe him. "No we don't, we look like we've been crossing mountains—and we have been crossing mountains. We look like explorers—and we are explorers. Beckett's even grown some whiskers on his chin."

Beckett tried to see his refection in the glass of the beer-house window.

Francie had nearly finished; she was just inking in the coast road. Joe went to try one of the bicycles when a hoarse yelp made him drop it. Three more of Monty's men were stumbling and limping towards them, Gervais and Monocle-Man among them. They each grabbed a bike, hauled themselves into the saddle and pedalled off slowly after the others.

"Clever," said Beckett. "Nine men, three bicycles. They all get a turn to ride."

Joe wondered what had happened to Baldy and the other man, and the rest of the mechanical horses.

Francie capped her pen and sat very still and pale.

Beckett blew on the map to hurry the ink dry then rolled it up with the others and pushed them into the tube. "Let's gallop."

The sun wasn't far above the horizon now. Joe helped Francie to her feet. She tottered for two steps then folded up like Ma's deck-chair. Humph shrieked and Joe looked around in panic.

"She needs a doctor. A hospital."

"I'll carry her," said Beckett.

He lifted her limp body over his shoulder, held onto her legs and strode off with her head and arms bouncing against his back. Sal piggybacked Humph, Joe carried the roll of maps in one hand and dragged the altimeter with the other and they ran after Beckett.

CHAPTER TWENTY-FOUR

THE END OF THE RACE

The shadows grew longer. They passed one of Monty's men shuffling along, exhausted. And another. Beckett paused to catch his breath and adjust Francie's weight, this time carrying her in his arms. Joe checked her breathing.

"Still alive." He could feel his heart thumping. How would they find a doctor? Was there a hospital in New Coalhaven?

"I can run," said Humph, and slid off Sal's back.

The first buildings of the town came into view. A hotel or two; a yard full of machinery; a giant gasometer, a coal-merchant. Did doctors put signs on their houses? Joe wanted to ask someone, but the place was deserted. Where was everybody?

They passed the rest of Monty's walking men.

The sun was setting. The sky was glowing orange. None of them had any breath left. They slowed to a limping walk.

And there, in a paddock behind a blacksmith's workshop, was a huge bustle of people, and smoke, delicious cooking smells and a banner declaring:

THE PEOPLE OF NEW COALHAVEN EXTEND
A WARM WELCOME TO ALL EXPLORERS

A man stood under the banner with a pocket watch and a gong. He began to call out: "Ten, nine ..."

Lots of voices joined in: "Eight, seven, six, five …"

"Quick!" Sal grabbed Humph's hand and Joe held on to a bit of Beckett's shirt and together they ran under the banner as the man shouted, "Two. One!"

A flag fell, the gong rang out and the race was over.

A shout went up, "The kiddies are here!"

"They said you was goners," said the man with the flag. "Mr Runcible! Mr Runcible! The kiddies are here!"

"Please," said Joe, "please, we need a doctor."

He'd been imagining Ma would rush to meet them, but there was no sign of her. He spotted Keith Skinner prowling about in the distance, and Sir Monty who was sitting rigid on his mechanical horse as if he were posing for his portrait. Somewhere nearby Cody Cole's voice boomed out, saying how much easier the whole race had been than he'd anticipated.

The Santander team was last to finish, but that didn't matter now. All that mattered was Francie.

The young woman didn't look old enough to be a doctor, but she promised Joe that she was fully qualified and worked at the New Coalhaven cottage hospital. She listened to Joe's story while she felt for Francie's pulse, and looked in her mouth and eyes. Joe didn't mention the flying but explained about the honey.

"Well, what are you waiting for?" said the doctor. "Go and find the cook, and beg."

So Joe did, and returned with a small bowl of honey. The doctor stirred some into a cup of hot water and spooned it into

Francie's mouth, while Joe squeezed her fingers and whispered, "We did it, Francie, we've finished! No more racing. Wake up now, come on."

He could sense her coming back towards him from a long way off. Her eyelids fluttered. She drank more of the warm honey.

With Francie declared recovering and not about to die, Sal and Beckett delivered their maps to Mr Molineux, the Regional Railway Manager, in his office, which was really a tent behind the marquee. He took Francie's maps and drawings from Sal and smiled condescendingly as he showed them out.

"Good show. Well done."

"But not well done enough," Sal said sadly when they were out of earshot. "I didn't want to be last. I really, really didn't." Francie being ill, and them coming last, and still no sign of Ma. It was a disaster.

"But at least we all finished, which some of the teams didn't. That's impressive." Beckett put an arm round her shoulder and gave her a hug. "You did a grand job."

Sal smiled. "So did you. We all did. Though I wish we could just get some dinner and keep walking. There are too many people here."

"Dinner! Just smell it!"

Someone walked past with a tray of pies, and there were two fires with meat roasting on spits above them. Sal stopped to examine the system of pulleys and chains that turned the spits.

"That's clever."

When she saw that Francie was sitting up and drinking a mug of soup in a quiet corner of the marquee, she burst into tears.

"Thank goodness!" She wiped her eyes on her sleeve, then she laughed. "I feel like a mountain path. Up and down, up and down. Francie is better and there's a feast. That's two ups, but what happens tomorrow? No mother. No money. No tent. We don't even have a hairbrush."

They were bustled off to the bath-house that was next to the blacksmith's shop, girls one way, boys the other. It was wonderful to wallow in a big tank of hot water, and wash their hair, and scrub themselves all over. But the pleasure was rather spoiled when they had to put their filthy clothes back on afterwards.

Beckett was their spokesperson. He was happy to answer everyone's questions about their adventures, and didn't seem to mind the bustling and jostling. Sal asked anyone who'd listen: "Is our mother here, yet?" But everyone just shrugged.

And it turned out that no one realised they'd done the whole expedition without an adult. Everyone thought they were looking for Ma because they'd run ahead of her across the line or lost her in the crowd. People exclaimed, "Well I never!" and, "Would you believe it!"

"Wait until they see Francie's maps," Sal whispered to Joe. "They'll treat us seriously, then."

Each team had its own table at the front of the marquee, near the dais, and the rest of the marquee was crowded with tables for officials and townspeople. The Santander table was nearest the entrance, and next to them grumpy Keith Skinner had a whole table to himself. Beyond, Monty's Mountaineers traded insults with the Cowboys on the far side. Sal would have liked to tell Cody Cole what she thought of him, but she was too tired.

Joe patted her hand. "One good thing: Monty and Cody Cole both know they've lost their money. They bet we wouldn't make it, but here we are."

The food was served straight away. There was soup, then meat and baked potatoes, followed by apple pie and chocolate cake. The Santander team ate in hungry silence. The marquee was illuminated by a string of hissing gas lanterns that cast crazy shadows on the canvas walls. Being in a hot, enclosed space with so much clatter and chatter made Sal feel as if the breath was being squeezed out of her. If she'd had any energy left she'd have run outside, back to the mountains, and kept on walking. What must Francie be feeling?

But Francie was ploughing happily through her cake.

Sal nudged her and waved her hand at all the people. "You all right?"

Francie nodded and pulled back her hair to reveal tufts of cotton wool sticking out of her ears.

"The doctor had it in her doctoring bag, so I asked her for some," said Joe. "Easy."

"Clever! Why didn't we think of that before." Sal propped her head on her hand. She was so tired, and so full.

Francie pushed her plate away, put her head down on her arms and shut her eyes. Sal folded her jersey up.

"Here." She slipped it under Francie's head. "We'll go soon."

She must have dropped off to sleep herself because she jerked awake to hear a loud woman's voice introducing herself as Miss Prowdy, the Mayor of New Coalhaven. The marquee had hushed. Miss Prowdy was a tall woman and the feathers in her hat brushed against the roof when she stood up.

"Welcome, everyone, and hearty congratulations to the four teams that have made it here to the finish line through all kinds of adventure. It will take some time for Mr Molineux's surveyors and engineers to compare the feasibility of the routes, so today we just have to reward the team that was first across the finish line."

Sal groaned. "So even if our maps are best we won't know for ages."

"Now, this is so exciting!" The mayor beamed at them all and put on a pair of spectacles to read from her notes. "The first person to arrive was Mr Keith Skinner, who entered the paddock last night, first by two short minutes!" The audience started to clap and Keith Skinner got to his feet looking very pleased.

But the mayor held up her hand for silence and looked solemn. She read on. "However, it seems that Mr Skinner was alone, and Rule 31 of the race handbook clearly states that a minimum of half the team must cross the finish line in a timely manner. Therefore, I am delighted to announce that Cody Cole and his Cowboys were the first team to finish, and they win five hundred golden guineas!"

The Cowboys cheered and Cody Cole rose and bowed to the crowd. Keith Skinner swore loudly and snatched up his knife and fork. He looked ready to chop the Cowboys into little pieces.

Cody Cole took the bag of money from Miss Prowdy and waved it at the crowd.

"I wish Ma was here," said Joe.

"Me too," said Sal. They'd done so much, and now it was over—and they had nothing to show for it. "What'll you do now?" she asked Beckett.

He shrugged. "Try for work as a miner, maybe. Or a stoker on a steamship. Earn a passage back home for me and the donkeys." He cut himself another slice of cake. "I'm not sorry, mind. Not sorry I came at all, even though we didn't win. It was a grand adventure."

Sal looked at Francie and Humph sleeping with their heads on the table, and she thought about the Cowboy who had kidnapped Humph, and how Francie had nearly died, and she thought about Beckett shovelling coal so he could return the donkeys to Mr Buckle. How come the adults could cheat and not work as a team and still win? Her face grew hotter, until she felt as if she might burst out of her skin. She jumped up, but she didn't shout or thump anything. Instead, she went to the door of the marquee, gulped down several big breaths of fresh air, then marched back inside and up to the table where Mr Molineux and Miss Prowdy were drinking coffee.

Her heart was threatening to choke her, but she swallowed hard and smiled politely.

"Excuse me," she said firmly. "I think there's something you ought to know."

CHAPTER TWENTY-FIVE

H IS FOR HUMPHREY

The Cowboys were making a great racket at their table, drinking beer and whisky and singing a song, the chorus of which went: "We won't listen to a word you say, there ain't no one gonna get in our way!"

Joe closed his eyes.

"One moment, please!" Miss Prowdy's voice forced Joe awake again. A spoon clattered on a plate. "Silence, please. We have just been alerted to a grave accusation." She cleared her throat. "I have been informed that Cody Cole's team of Cowboys gained an advantage over the Santander family by kidnapping one of their team members. Can this be true?"

Everyone started shouting. Sal was standing next to the mayor. Cody Cole was on his feet, hands hovering near the revolvers in his holsters.

"Slander!"

Mr Molineux stood up. "We'll see about that, Mr Cole. Is this Humphrey?" He strode over to the table and shook Humph's shoulder. Humph sat up, looking confused and grumpy at being woken. Mr Molineux took his hand and yanked him up onto the dais.

"Careful!" said Sal.

"Quiet," barked Mr Molineux. "This is a serious accusation. Tell me exactly what happened, little boy."

Humphrey stuck his thumb in his mouth, closed his eyes and leaned against Mr Molineux's leg.

"Don't go back to sleep, Humph," Beckett's low voice cut through the clamour. "Tell them. Tell them about the bad man and the horse."

There was a lot of shushing, the marquee quietened, and everyone sat forward to listen.

"We ain't kidnappers!" snarled Cody Cole.

Humph's eyes popped open. "One of you is." He looked around and pointed. "That one. That one who's still got his hat on. He picked me up and rode me on his horse and tied me up and put me in his cave but I escaped and Francie helped me."

Cody Cole looked furious but managed a dismissive laugh. "Hokum! The boy's listened to too many stories. None of my men has been anywhere near 'em."

Humphrey narrowed his eyes. Joe knew that look; he exchanged a hopeful glance with Francie, who had woken up and was listening with her hands clasped in front of her mouth.

"Never?" said Humph.

"None of them. Ever," said Cody Cole.

"Then how come I know that he—" Humph pointed at the man with the hat, "has freckles like a big H here?" He pointed to his forearm. "Which actually I know cos he had his arm around me on the horse and his sleeve was scrunched up and all I could see was a freckly H and lots of hairiness. And H is for Humphrey and H is for hair and for hat, which I know because I AM NEARLY FIVE AND I AM NOT STUPID!"

"H is for home!" squawked Carrot, waking up and strutting across the table.

"Pull back your sleeve! Reveal your arm!" demanded Miss Prowdy, but the man in the hat was already trying to get away. He didn't have a chance. Lots of people launched themselves into his path and many voices shouted that he did indeed have an H in freckles.

Then Joe noticed that Cody Cole was trying to slip towards the exit unnoticed.

"Stop him! Stop him!" he shouted.

And there were Agatha Amersham and Zinnia, Harriet and Daphne forming a solid wall in the doorway. Cody Cole tried to shove Zinnia out of the way but Agatha and Daphne grabbed an arm each and flipped him onto the floor. They pinned his arms, Joe and Beckett threw themselves onto his back and Daphne and Zinnia each sat on a kicking leg. Mr Molineux wrenched the bag of gold from his fingers.

After Agatha and her team had been welcomed, and the Cowboys had been marched off to the lock-up, Joe found he wasn't tired any more. Agatha's team sat at the Santanders' table and Joe cut chocolate cake for everyone.

"Three cheers for Humph! What a great noticer you are!"

Sal scooped him onto her lap and hugged him. "You're a champion!"

"Three cheers for Sal, too," said Beckett.

Sal flushed. "I hate being a tell-tale. But we've all done such hard things to get here. Those men were cruel and they cheated. They didn't deserve a prize. And I remembered what you said about the ink. There's no harm in asking."

They told the story to the women explorers, who were suitably shocked. Agatha was just starting to tell Sal about scholarships when the officials, who had been sitting with their heads together, stood up. Miss Prowdy tapped a spoon on a glass and called for silence again.

"The next team to arrive were Sir Monty's Mountaineers. However, only four of them crossed the finish line before sunset, which is less than half their team. So, the prize purse for the first—and only—team to arrive in sufficient numbers and *without cheating* goes to the Santander family. Congratulations, Santanders!"

The whole marquee erupted in cheering.

Miss Prowdy beckoned them all to come up to the dais and shook their hands. The crowd hushed. "These remarkable children have succeeded where the adults failed. Tell us, Sal, how did you do it?"

Sal considered. "I think it's because we're a very good team. You know, we stuck together, and we helped each other." She looked at Sir Monty and Keith Skinner. "We needed all of us, including Humphrey and even Carrot, our parrot. And we laughed a lot. And also," she added, because she felt she should be as truthful as she could, "we were lucky."

Miss Prowdy said how delighted she was, and gave Sal the heavy bag of gold. Five hundred golden guineas!

A reporter from the *Gazette* asked a beaming Sal what they were going to do with the money.

"We're going to look for our father," she told him. "And our mother. We're going to find our parents."

Mrs Baddeley's spare room had two big feather beds, and a trundle bed for Humph.

"Oh, bliss," murmured Sal as she snuggled down beside Francie, with the bag of gold between them. "I'm buying everyone a feather bed if there's any money left over."

"A telescope," said Joe.

"New boots," said Beckett.

"Sausages," mumbled Humphrey.

"Do you remember wishing on the new moon a month ago?" said Joe. "Humph wanted a story and he got his wish, and Francie wanted to touch snow. Beckett wanted the railway to go to his village. Three wishes out of five. Not bad. No more days to go."

Joe slept and slept, until the smell of new-baked bread penetrated his dreams and he opened his eyes. Bright sun streamed through the curtains. There was Humph, eyes shut, thumb in. There was Beckett's hair sticking up above the sheet. There was Sal, lying on her back, but no Francie.

236

Heart thumping, he padded down the stairs and found his way to the kitchen.

And there was Francie, in one of Mrs Baddeley's enormous nighties, and she was sitting on Ma's lap!

Joe threw himself at his mother and they clung together, laughing and crying in a three-way hug. Then the others heard the noise and piled in, everyone squealing and exclaiming.

"Oh, my giddy aunt!" said Mrs Baddeley, dabbing at her face with a dishcloth. "We've not had this much excitement since the goat got on the roof!"

Then Humphrey noticed what Mrs Baddeley was making. "Pancakes!"

They explained to Ma that they had a lot of catch-up eating to do, and tucked into lunchtime breakfast.

"I was so worried," she said. "You had no money for food."

"But we had Beckett," said Joe, "And now we all know how to make bread and porridge and lots of things."

Ma hugged Beckett. She kept shaking her head and her eyes watered.

"A woman in Grand Prospect tried to make us pay for food she said you'd ordered. She shouted and spat at us," said Sal, "but I promised her you'd pay."

"I saw her and I paid her."

"Thank goodness! That was my last worry."

"Oh, Sal!" Ma squeezed her hand.

Carrot flew in through the back door and landed on Ma's shoulder. She pecked her cheek. "How you, Missus?"

"So glad to see you, Carrot!" Ma stroked Carrot's back.

"She saved Joe's life," said Beckett. "She's a champion life-saving parrot."

Ma pulled out her hanky and had a good blow.

"What happened to you?" asked Sal through a mouthful of pancake.

Ma told how it had taken her many days to get to Grand Prospect, only to discover that they'd gone on without her.

"I was so scared," she said. "I kept imagining you falling off cliffs, or drowning, or getting lost or hypothermia."

"That all happened," said Beckett, "except Joe only nearly drowned."

"And we only nearly got eaten by a bear," said Sal.

"Oh, my word!" Mrs Baddeley hugged her tea towel to her chest.

"And Humph was kidnapped, and Francie was unconscious," said Joe.

Ma shook her head in horror. "But you got here! Are you really all right? Really? I'm so proud of you. All of you."

"We got here, and we won!" said Joe. "Five hundred golden guineas."

"What?!" Ma's mouth fell open and she looked around at the others to see if he was teasing her.

"It's true." Sal wiped a trickle of syrup off her chin. "I thought they'd have told you already. We've got a bag of gold upstairs."

"Now we can go and look for Pa," said Humph.

Ma shook her head and wiped her eyes with her knuckles. "What extraordinary children."

"What did you do when you found we'd started the race without you?" asked Joe.

"I went as far as Beckett's village and heard about the donkeys and which way you'd gone. But Beckett's mother said you were very organised and being sensible, and by then you were over a week ahead of me. So," she drank some tea, "I decided to trust you. I went back to Grand Prospect and took a berth on a ship going to New Coalhaven. But a terrible storm blew up. The ship was blown so far off course that we've only just got here, many days late. I was sure you'd all be blown right off the mountains."

"We nearly were, but Humph spotted a cave just in time," said Joe.

Humphrey was concentrating on spreading strawberry jam right to the edges of a slice of fresh bread. Ma hugged him. "Clever, clever Humphrey!"

"There were bats in it," said Humph.

"We watched whole trees blow past," said Sal. "It was the craziest thing."

Beckett and Joe wandered up the road behind Sal, and Francie and Humph trailed behind them, wearing seaweed crowns. They'd been to the beach. It was too cold and dirty for swimming but they'd built a sand tower, dug a moat, and messed around for the whole afternoon. It had been good to get away from the noise of the town and curious people, and even from the watchful eyes of Ma for a little while. She kept wanting to brush their hair. She even talked of starting lessons again.

Beckett loved his shiny new boots but Joe's new trousers and shirt were still uncomfortably stiff. Tomorrow he and Francie and Beckett were going to fetch the donkeys from the farm and Joe planned to wear his old clothes. He couldn't wait to be off walking again. After that, Beckett and the donkeys would be getting a boat back to Brightwater Village, which everyone was sad about. Mr Arbuckle would be happy to see his donkeys, though. And surprised. And Beckett's family would be excited to see him. They'd be astonished when he showed them his new purse full of gold.

"What will you buy first?" Joe asked Beckett.

"First off?" Beckett tipped back his top hat. "Tools and

materials to mend our house. Then a milk cow, and then? Then, I'm going to buy a traction engine."

"But they're so noisy!" said Joe.

"They're noisy machines that can do anything. When the railway building begins, I'll rent it out to the railway company then my family will always have money."

Joe marvelled. Beckett was already thinking of the time beyond tomorrow.

"There are visitors," Sal warned them from the gate.

Two people were bustling up Mrs Baddeley's path, calling out to Ma who was sitting in the sun on the veranda.

It was Miss Prowdy, looking excited, and Mr Molineux, puffed up with importance. Ma shook hands with them; Francie hid behind Ma's chair.

"News!" said Miss Prowdy, stroking the mayoral chain. "Extraordinary news. You—"

"Are winners!" interrupted Mr Molineux. "The Santander team were first home. But now you have also been declared winners of the best route. Furthermore, your maps and accompanying drawings are apparently exemplary. My surveyor is of the belief that your route is as well considered as any he has ever seen, and the railway company will be adopting it in its entirety. In total, you have won three thousand five hundred golden guineas."

"Guineas!" shrieked Carrot, flying in circles.

"Yes! The railway will go through my village!" Beckett sat down with a bump on the step.

"Three cheers for us!" Joe grabbed Humph's hands and swung him round and round, laughing and kicking his legs out.

"If we give Mr Arbuckle a hundred, and you get a quarter, you'll get eight hundred and fifty guineas, Beckett," said Sal.

"Shouldn't it be a fifth? Anyway," Beckett said slowly, "it's all thanks to Francie, really. Her maps are a miracle of pencil work. And Sal's clever calculations. And Joe's route-finding."

"And your cooking. We'd never have survived without you being in charge of food," said Sal.

Ma drew Francie out from behind the chair and hugged her close. She dripped tears into Francie's hair. "That's an unimaginable amount of money. It was our last chance, but now—well, anything is possible."

"Question is, is it enough money to buy some mountains as well as going to find Pa?" said Joe. "I don't know how much mountains cost, but me and Francie would like to buy some, so that they don't all get dug up for gold, and coal, and roads and towns. Some of them can stay like they are for the eagles and the bears."

"And the silver wolf," said Humphrey, stretching his arms out wide. "We mustn't ever forget the silver wolf."